A Cratchit Family Christmas

A NOVEL

Val,

Merry Christmas 2016

Paul Mast

Paul Mast

ISBN: 1537457462
ISBN 13: 9781537457468
Library of Congress Control Number: 2016914757
CreateSpace Independent Publishing Platform
North Charleston, South Carolina

Preface

" A Christmas Carol" by Charles Dickens was published and released on December 19, 1843. No one has written a sequel; neither shall I. Ebenezer Scrooge is a story book character who is so revered in literary history that he has earned a place in the hallowed lore of reader's imaginations. Scrooge is a marble bust sitting nobly on a pedestal in a statuary hall surrounded by other mythological icons created from the sophisticated imagination of literary genius's. A time-honored sign hangs from the pedestal, *"Do Not Touch."*

My imagination was teased with crafting a tale around the character of Bob Cratchit, Scrooge's kind-hearted and dependable clerk. Though he played a minor role it was enough for me to contemplate how to bring his character into the light as central to a story spun from the threads of Scrooge's Christmas Eve conversion, the event that allowed Scrooge to exit and for Bob Cratchit to take the powerful story in a new direction.

In the crafting and writing process, I had a conversion experience which parallels that of Scrooge. At first, Bob Cratchit was only a name hewn from the pages of a Dickens novella, but as I owned the truth that I did not create him, his voice spoke to my imagination. Gradually he developed as a main character, along with his wife and their three children, who immortalize the best of his steady temperament and generous nature. As this process unfolded Bob and I became friends.

A Cratchit Family Christmas is set in the late 1800's. The story begins with the death and funeral of Mr. Scrooge. While Dickens's imagination divided his story into three parts, each based on a revealing spirit who visited Scrooge my story is framed within the context of the active ingenuities of the Cratchit family. Bob and Alice Cratchit and their children harnessed their best practices in late Victorian England and gave credibility to the memory of their adopted 'Uncle Scrooge."

In so doing, the post-Scrooge Cratchit family, create their own legacy by weaving the inheritance their forever-changed adopted uncle left each of them, into their caring and selfless values as a family. Scrooge's philanthropy to the Cratchit family, in the form of lavish investments and dowries, enabled them to forge their own legacy by their outreach to the poor, the homeless, abandoned children, pensioners, prodigals estranged from families and immigrants seeking refuge in an ever-growing and highly industrialized England.

It is my hope that you will befriend the Cratchit family as I did through their family traditions and values. May they inspire all to imagine new ways for nurturing your own family ties and our life legacies.

CHAPTER 1

The Funeral of Ebenezer Scrooge

*E*benezer Scrooge's funeral was not a mournful event. If members of the press in attendance had come to report on who wept the loudest and who grieved the most, they left sadly disappointed.

Little did everyone know, except his family, that the deceased had planned every detail, except the day and time of his death? Providence chose that, making his post-Christmas passing the reason the undertaker posed a pleasantly contented expression on the face of the deceased. Ever since his Christmas Eve conversion of 1850, Scrooge and Christmas had been the best of friends with the season turning him into the Pied Piper of West London and replacing his former "Bah Humbug!" with "Merry Christmas." Instead of scolding the advocates of the poor and needy who came around asking for charity at this special time of year, he welcomed their visits and responded with generous donations. The old Scrooge - a mean spirited pinchpenny had been miraculously transformed into a kind-hearted benefactor and a genuine friend to many.

Those for whom the former Scrooge was a distinct memory laughed at his alteration, concluding that it was merely cosmetic. He let them laugh, for he was wise enough to know those who had never experienced a personal conversion were spiritually blind to those who had. So he let them wrinkle up their eyes, form grins and laugh at his newly acquired effervescent and child-like behavior. The smile that rested on his own heart validated his conversion and inspired him how to create unique ways to keep the spirit of Christmas all year through.

The detractors and doubters of the new Scrooge were few among the large gathering of mourners. Scrooge broke every protocol in planning his own funeral. Instead of being waked in the parlor of his renovated three story town house in the Mayfair section of London, he combined his wake with the funeral at the Church of St. Martin-in-the-Fields. The neoclassical edifice was constructed between 1772 and 1776.

The reformed Scrooge carefully chose this site as his place of worship. He knew that the story of the saintly fourth century Martin of Tours paralleled his own conversion experience. Born into a noble French military family Martin was the son of a veteran. Legend has it that he once came upon a naked beggar. His heart was pierced with compassion. He used his sword to cut his military cape into two pieces and gave half to the beggar for clothing. St. Martin of Tours and Ebenezer Scrooge have been soul mates for twenty years. They bond every time Scrooge visits the iconic Anglican Church anchored on the northeast corner of Trafalgar Square.

Ever since his Christmas Eve conversion in 1850, Scrooge has been a friend to beggars. He once gave his coat, scarf and gloves to several frozen beggars on a bitter cold winter street. Modest in his storytelling he once hinted to Bob Cratchit, "They keep my new heart full of compassion which fuels my reformed life."

Prior to his somewhat mystical spiritual transformation, Scrooge was not a religious man. He worshipped the god of money. But after his transformation he made spiritual connections between his newly grounded rebirth and the birth of the child born in Bethlehem whose presence he began to encounter in the poor and needy. For more years than he could remember, he chided one of the Christmas spirits who visited him with the words, "go and redeem someone younger and more promising." In the end it was his redemption the spirits pursued and achieved.

During the last twenty years of his life, Scrooge practiced a faith that was childlike. His adult relationship with the Christ child kept him humble and playful. He enjoyed teasing God to use his good fortune to partner with the Savior in helping the lame to walk the blind to see and the hungry to be fed. His spiritually renewed life echoed the lyrics of John Newton's classic hymn, "Amazing Grace." For that reason he chose it as the gathering song for his funeral.

The four hundred people in attendance were invited not to grieve his passing, but to celebrate his life. Scrooge left specific instructions that his casket be closed. He disliked the practice of people filing by like window shoppers and whispering to one another, "He makes a lovely corpse." Also, he considered the ritual of congratulating an undertaker for shaving ten years off the face of a seventy year old man, through the wonders of cosmetics, to be a wasted compliment.

He wrote in his instructions, "Face powder helps the living to smile at one another. I can't smile back in a coffin, so don't waste it on me."

Instead of gazing on him in death, saying things about him he couldn't refute, Scrooge preferred people to share stories of their life- enriching relationships with him. He wanted mourners to hear the first-hand testimonies from those who validated his conversion, thereby achieving in some way what Scrooge himself could not. He had a hidden and sincere motive, hoping that such oral affirmations would turn his funeral into a conversion experience for those who were still disbelievers.

His nephew Fred, the only child of his adoring sister, Fanny, who died in childbirth, served as a Master of Ceremonies. Estranged for twenty years, their reconciliation was one of the first fruits of Scrooge's Christmas Eve conversion.

Fred stood confidently in the center aisle of the barrel-vaulted church. His eyes surveyed the faces of mourners. Those in the galleries perched forward to hear his words. Removing a grey velvet glove, he rested one hand gently on the coffin of his deceased uncle, while occasionally referring to handwritten notes he held in the other hand. He set the tone speaking in a lively and lyrical manner.

"For most of my adult life, I went by Uncle Ebenezer's office every December 24th to wish him a Merry Christmas and invite him to Christmas dinner. For all those years he retorted with his now-famous phrase, 'Christmas is a Bah Humbug.' Thanks to inheriting my mother's pleasant nature I never let my uncle's miserable soul infect my happy spirit."

Pausing for some dramatic effect, he continued.

"Then twenty years ago, on Christmas Day, to the surprise of everyone, he appeared at my house, embraced my wife, asked her forgiveness for his stubbornness and joined us in making merry. It was obvious to me and our guests that he was a changed man. Instead of asking questions about the new behaviors and the similarly new attitude towards the season of Christmas, my wife happily swept him off his feet as he joined her in a polka. We all clapped in rhythm."

"Uncle," I said, "I never knew you could dance." Wearing a pleasant smile, he replied, nearly breathless, "Neither did I."

His syncopated steps were all the proof I needed to confirm that his penitent heart was beating with new unprecedented joy. The new cheerful presence he emitted that Christmas day was the best Christmas gift I've ever received."

Clearing a slight unsteadiness in his voice, he added, "Nothing has been comparable to it since."

"This is the kind of storytelling my uncle requested at his funeral. I know it is unconventional, but it is in keeping with the true wishes of an eccentric accountant, philanthropist, friend and mentor we have known the past twenty years."

Fred noticed that the faces of some mourners were painted with frowns, thinking that such a novel practice was irreverent at a funeral service in tradition-laced Victorian England. Other faces, however, were glazed with smiles that signaled pleasant approval. He locked onto the latter faces as he harnessed the courage to continue.

"One of the best things I liked about my converted Uncle Scrooge was his new sense of humor. In his own words, he asked me to explain to all of you that he wanted storytelling at his funeral so we would avoid ridiculing Shakespeare's line in *Much Ado about Nothing,* 'Done to death by slanderous tongue.'"

"I clearly recall that one evening a few months ago, we were chatting in his parlor, enjoying his favorite port, when he surprised me by saying that one daily ritual he will be free of when he dies is reading obituaries."

Fred waited for the laughter to subside before adding, "It was so unrehearsed that, during my laughter, I nearly choked on the port."

As vibrant chuckles echoed throughout the vaulted church, Fred stepped aside to allow as his adoring wife Catherine, to take his place beside the coffin.

"Uncle Ebenezer has made us so happy these past twenty years. He is the godfather of our son, Fred, Jr. We couldn't ask for a better person to fulfill that role. His weekly visits for Sunday dinner made the Lord's Day a double portion of blessings. His role as babysitter for his godson during his childhood years turned our uncle into our special 'Governess,' or as Fred, Jr., called him his 'Governor.'

Wiping tears from her eyes, she took a deep breath to regain her composure.

"We feel his presence in our cocker spaniel, a gift to Fred, Jr. on his fourth birthday. The spirit of Uncle Ebenezer is near every time we call out "Ebie" and he comes running full of a puppy's love to lick us and cheer us.

"In addition to never forgetting our winter-into-springtime birthdays, he surprised us with gifts for the winter, spring and summer solstices, resolving that they should be holidays to close the gaps between Christmas and Easter."

She paused to ponder her words. "I could say so much more about him, but instead I'll let others say it." She returned to the pew and snuggled in between her husband and son.

As if on cue, Bob and Alice Cratchit eagerly rose and stepped forward. Bob's soft manner of speaking was a noticeable contrast to Catherine's jovial voice. Dressed in a traditional mourning suit, Bob's poise and polished cadence of speech commanded attention.

"As most of you know, I worked for Mr. Scrooge for thirty years. Or should I say I worked for two Mr. Scrooge's. The first ten years I clerked for a man who was stingy, mean-spirited and blessed with an over- abundance of repute for offending people."

Muffled laughter spread through the congregation. Others silently shook their heads in agreement.

He turned toward the closed coffin and bowed respectfully.

"I know he won't curse me for saying that because I honestly spoke those same words to him often after his Christmas Eve conversion of 1850."

"The first Mr. Scrooge was not a pleasant man to work for. I never considered him to be an Employer of the Year."

Bob Cratchit waited for the muted laughter to subside.

"Then, twenty years ago, he experienced a spiritual transformation. To this very day, I consider it to be some kind of miracle. It was as if a good spirit got inside him, wrestled the old mean spirit to the ground and emerged victorious as the new spirit. The new Mr. Scrooge proved to be true to his word, bearing witness by treating everyone with respect, being a benefactor to worthy causes. He generously helped with the medical expenses for my youngest son, Tim, who was stricken at a young age with a serious physical disability."

Everyone in attendance knew the story of Scrooge's special affection for Tim Cratchit, and knew that he would soon share his own testimony.

"From the first Mr. Scrooge I learned how to add, subtract and manage a ledger with intimidation and fear. On more than one occasion, while auditing my entries he found an error of one penny farthing. The next morning, that pinchpenny boss called out my mistake. That was the Mr. Scrooge who lived by the ledger, whose values in life were limited to debit and credit columns. He lived to balance books and to exact interest from debtors."

"From the transformed Mr. Scrooge, I learned how to become free of fear, how to cheerfully balance work with family life. I learned, that respecting clients, leads to appreciating accounting as respectable work. I learned the difference between being stingy from being ethical."

With those words Bob Cratchit, with a slight bow of his head, acknowledged the presence of the Prime Ministers' Chancellor of the Exchequer seated behind his family. This high treasury official evidenced the clout that Ebenezer Scrooge maintained with the British government.

"Ten years ago, Mr. Scrooge paid me the highest respect by dissolving the firm of Scrooge & Marley, and establishing new bylaws forming the firm of Scrooge & Cratchit. He was a true mentor in smoothing my transition from a clerk to a partner. Two years ago he surprised me again by appointing me the overseer of his philanthropic causes. During those years he taught me that good leaders inspire us to put confidence in them, but great leaders inspire us to put confidence in ourselves."

The congregation clung to every word Bob Cratchit spoke. Their attention and awe were silent indicators of approval that their loans, debts and investments were in safe hands during this time of transition.

"In closing, let me say that as I visited with Mr. Scrooge four days before his passing, I asked him to share anything he wanted me to say at his funeral. In a nearly inaudible voice, he smiled and fulfilled my request, 'Say not that I had a lovely funeral. Say instead that I hope everyone never misses a year, a month or even a day to live a fulfilled life.' Before I could assure him, he winked and added 'and 'say that I wish them a Merry Christmas.'"

The last line evoked smiles. Everyone knew that Ebenezer Scrooge died on the feast of St. Stephen, the day after Christmas. What they didn't know was that, for the first time in his life, he downsized his Christmas decorations in his modestly furnished townhouse. Bob kept to himself the strange intuition that somehow Scrooge knew this was his final Christmas on earth. After his burial, it became known that most of his decorations that year had been shipped to the Holy Child House he founded for orphaned children in east London.

Once again it seemed that he had been visited by a mysterious Christmas spirit, and, his transformed and compliant heart made it easy for that spirit to accomplish its mission.

Bob deferred to his wife, Alice, proudly standing by his side. Her unconventional attire would be the talk of ladies' circles long after the funeral. Instead of a traditional black mourning dress with lace and flowing veils, Alice Cratchit wowed the assembly with a ladies burgundy Edwardian suit. A classic white Gibson girl blouse was accented at the neck with a deluxe floppy bow tie. The jacket and unhooped skirt were etched with a thin black trim. Black ankle books protruded from underneath the skirt which was cut at least ten inches from the floor. A matching burgundy boater hat topped her perfectly angled head like a royal crown. Two modest pieces of black ribbon streamed down the nape of her neck. Only her daughter Martha, the owner of two milliner stores in central London, thought her mother's cutting edge attire, added sparkle and grace to the occasion. She also knew the deceased would approve and would say as much if he weren't the corpse.

"I did not initially have the level of tolerance or respect that my good husband had for Mr. Scrooge. But my heart warmed to him many years ago after I witnessed the diverse ways his heart warmed for others. My conversion was complete when he asked me to collaborate with him in establishing an Alms House here at St. Martin's."

Alice Cratchit became more animated as her skill as a storyteller became more rhythmic.

"Once the Alms House was dedicated and open, I was edified how Mr. Scrooge became happily involved in the day-to-day operations. His regular visits gave hope to the poor and destitute as he engaged them with great respect. Watching him was like learning the fine art of how to turn compassion into storytelling. He imparted a special glow whenever he served the street people in the food line. It left me with a sense that he was being fed with blessings he didn't deserve, but humbly welcomed."

Alice went on for five minutes cataloguing the virtues and selfless behaviors of the converted Mr. Scrooge. She garnered everyone's attention when she mentioned how her own sometimes restless heart was calmed and healed by his contented heart, especially the easy manner he displayed listening to people's woes.

"Whenever that happened, I felt as if I were catching pieces of the spirit that transformed him into a new man that celebrated Christmas Eve."

Pausing to add her own style of drama, she concluded,

"Watching him being so patient and gentle with the less fortunate transformed me. And the spirit of Christmas came alive in me no matter what time of year."

As Bob and Alice Cratchit returned to their pew, Peter Crachit stepped into the aisle.

The eldest child of Bob and Alice, Peter was the first to benefit from Scrooge's inner transformation. As soon as he completed secondary school, Scrooge paid the tuition for Peter's education in Finance and Accounting at the London City College. Little did the young, but ambitious honor student know that his benefactor was grooming him for future employment at the firm of Scrooge & Marley.

Following his life-changing Christmas Eve conversion, Scrooge sensed that God had a larger plan in mind for the transformed loan shark. That plan included mentoring younger employees who would carry on Scrooge's business dealings with the new desire to grow people's hearts as he helped to grow their financial investments. The more people invested their money with his firm, the more money they designated for charities. This inspired Scrooge to make growing people's hearts his legacy. Peter Cratchit was the insurance policy that would reap dividends for honoring Scrooge's philanthropic memory long after his passing.

In Peter Cratchit, Scrooge found someone who balanced fair business practices with balanced accounts, thus making him an asset in modeling the kind of trust in financial institutions where people ultimately trusted their money.

It helped that Peter was cut from the loins of his father, Scrooge's trustworthy and fiercely devoted office clerk. After his transformation, the pinchpenny boss did not hesitate to tell Bob Cratchit that enduring ten years of his insufferable behavior made Bob worthy of being canonized a saint. The self-effacing clerk had displayed his trademark humility in his response: "Even saints have threads of sinfulness in them, Mr. Scrooge."

Standing next to the coffin of his benefactor, the six foot disciple of the deceased, shed a dignified and noble presence. At thirty-four years of age, his poise exuded a confidence beyond his years and his voice garnered singular attention.

"I am Peter Cratchit, a junior partner at the firm of Scrooge & Cratchit."

Tilting his head slightly to the right to acknowledge the deceased's living nephew, Fred, he morphed into sentimentality.

"I am also an adopted nephew of the deceased whom I have affectionately called 'Uncle Scrooge' for the past twenty years."

Refocusing his attention back on the assembly he continued.

"I was fourteen years old when stories of the miserly Mr. Scrooge first circulated among the neighbors in Camden Town. Instead of peddling in gossip, my father practiced silence over slander. A virtue higher than simple fear of losing his job commanded him to refrain from gossip. That virtue of self-respect enabled me to practice charity toward my father's employer's vices long before they became noticeable virtues."

At this accolade, Peter turned toward his father and beamed a wide smile. With a slight bow of the head his esteemed dad mirrored it back. It was a gesture that underscored the adage, *like father, like son.*

Bob Cratchit was filled with immense pride listening to his eldest. Peter had grown into a gentleman. The black Regency tailcoat with velvet trim which he wore for the funeral framed him as a distinguished gentleman. The finishing touch was the tan Giles double-breasted vest neatly tailored over a Tombstone white shirt with a perfectly tied black ascot. A classic watch and chain in antique black finish lobbed elegantly from the vest pocket. The black brushed cotton trousers and black leather shoes capped his regal stature.

"I was fifteen when I first met Mr. Scrooge. He visited our home the first Christmas after his life-changing conversion, so my first encounter was not with the man most people feared. On the contrary, his presence emitted a fine combination of cheerfulness and docility. He showed keen interest in our schooling and peppered me, particularly, with questions about my excellence in math."

Pivoting his head with a half-moon movement in order to survey the entire congregation, he added, in a tone of humor,

"I didn't know then as I know now what that veiled interest was all about."

The assembly caught his drift and laughed appropriately.

"He gifted our family that year, and every year afterwards with a turkey for Christmas dinner. He presented me and my siblings with two kinds of gifts. One gift was writing utensils, bonded paper and notebooks for school....much needed items that were critical for our education. The other gift, neatly wrapped in Christmas paper, was to be given away to a friend, neighbor or classmate less fortunate than us. Martha and I gave our gifts to two children down the street whose father was out work due to poor health. They were wide-eyed with surprise. After they said 'thank you' we followed Uncle Scrooge's instructions that if anyone asked who the gift was from, just say, 'From Santa who asked us to be his elves and deliver them for him.'"

"My siblings and I learned to cherish how much our adopted uncle enjoyed playing Santa Claus anonymously through our charitable outreach. It became a new style of St. Nick that we have continued to practice with own children."

"It didn't take long for Uncle Scrooge to feel at home whenever he visited our house. The impulse to share Christmas gifts with the less fortunate has made a home in us year after year, and we continue that sacred outreach in our ways with our own families. We are honored to keep alive the spirit of Christmas all year through. Suffice to say we had a good teacher."

Peter spoke gratefully, acknowledging Scrooge's generosity in paying for his college education then hiring him as a junior clerk upon his graduation.

"On my first day of work, he called me and my father into his office. Pouring three snifters of brandy, he toasted the end of my schooling and the beginning of my career at his firm. He raised his glass and paid my father a gracious compliment, 'I am doubly contented having two Cratchits as employees.'"

That sentimental memory triggered some unsteadiness in Peter. He regained his composure and joyfully introduced his sister.

"My sister Martha now has her own story to share."

Martha Cratchit, still single at thirty-two, is the only adopted niece of Uncle Ebenezer Scrooge. She calls herself a 'post-Victorian woman.' After secondary school, she went to work as a sales lady in an upscale milliner shop along London's fashionable Oxford Street. Her sharp mind, warm personality and superior attention to details earned her many promotions. She turned her business skills into good fortune and, making good on a loan from Scrooge, is now the proud owner of two respectable milliner and clothing shops for women. Her clientele includes royalty, wives of members of Parliament and scores of fashionable women from the toney residential Squares of London. Unknown to her high society clients, Martha sneaks away from her office every Wednesday afternoon to surprise poor children in the east side docks area of London with bonnets and ribbons, dolls and toys that make each of them feel special. As she is filled with joy brightening their day, she playfully muses to herself that she is Ebenezer Scrooge in a dress, a bonnet, and a perpetually cheerful face.

Her choice of clothing for Scrooge's funeral was intended to make both her and the deceased look good. Martha Cratchit made public appearances that were subtly intended as a fashion statement. This funeral was no exception. Ebenezer Scrooge himself coached his adopted niece in how to dress. The private conversations between the two in the days leading to his death, now secretly enshrined in the pages of her diary illustrate his influence on her manner and style.

"With my diary in hand I'd like to share with everyone the private conversation I had ten days ago."

"Today I visited with Uncle Ebenezer. He is now confined to bed, frail of health but pretending to be strong of spirit. He frets too much about all the attention from nurses and doctors. As always, he is grateful for Mrs. Dilber's fine management of his house and staff. He revealed having a strong sense that this may be his last Christmas. I recoiled hearing this thought, but recovered quickly to comfort him. He opened the door on the subject of his funeral with warmth and ease. Such a topic is avoided and frowned upon in this day and time, but Uncle Scrooge invited me into his confidence as easily as he held my hand tenderly. I sat on the edge of the bed and relished his company, with the sound of his breathing fading in and out.

He expressed his pride in supporting and guiding my career as an independent business woman. He thanked me again, as he has done many times before, for turning his loan of one thousand British Pounds into two successful stores. He reminded me again that he took that risk not to earn compounded interest, but to provide me an opportunity to establish a successful business. His face spoke esteem while mine revealed gratitude. He the benefactor, and I the entrepreneur, shared an intimate moment without words. Our expressions conveyed what the economy of words could not."

Martha paused to wipe a tear from her eyes before sharing more from her diary.

"I cracked a smile when he broached the subject of how he wanted me to dress for his funeral. I replied, with candid humor, that people would come to see him and not me. It was then that I discovered that he planned to be waked in a closed coffin. He went on to succinctly explain that he did not want his funeral to be a memorial service for him. Rather, he wanted it to focus on his legacy; how his charity and philanthropy will live on in the people who believed in his life-changing conversion many Christmas Eve's ago and who nurtured the new and kind and charitable Scrooge to life with their patience and understanding. He thanked me for being one of them while referencing the biblical passage from Matthew 21:16, *"From the lips of children and infants you, Lord, have called forth your praise."*

"A visionary man in every sense of the word, he quietly expressed his hope that I would live into the next millennium and that my attire for his funeral should express a smooth transition from the era of Queen Victoria to the surprises of the twentieth century. Be bold and be a leader for women he said, especially those who have suffered too long without their own voices and champions to cheer them on. When he spoke those words I felt them being etched on my soul. I caught his meaning and took to heart his subtle courage to get more involved in the Suffrage movement. My business mentor had turned into a kind of spiritual guide, quietly coaching me to move from the edges to the center; to put my trust in a higher power and become a voice for the rights of women as I have been a lone professional at the cutting edge of women's apparel."

"I left his house today comforted more by him than vice versa. I wondered if his words were a valedictory; not in the sense of a farewell oratory but, as a pep talk between uncle and niece, mentor and seeker, endearing friends and business confidantes. Our holy hour will assure me of a peaceful nights rest." Martha adjusted her focus away from the diary."

"This was the last entry before his passing on December 26th. The next day I honored his request and planned my attire for turning a funeral into fodder for someone's gossip column."

If Martha could peak into the casket she was sure her Uncle Ebenezer would be wearing an approving smile for her funeral attire, a dark brown corduroy suit with a tailored skirt. The long-lean cut jacket had a hemline that turned up at the sides. An elegant cameo chemisette framed in brass highlighted the neckline of her silk blouse that was a gift from her adopted uncle when she opened her first store. In place of a grieving veil, Martha wore a black satin teardrop hat.

Every woman in the congregation took notice. If her clothes could speak they would say, 'I can make every one of you look this good.' The business woman in Martha wondered how many new customers she might garner from her appearance at this funeral. She playfully marveled how her deceased adopted uncle might have stirred a pleasant smile on her heart.

"My best memory of Uncle Scrooge," deferring respectfully to Fred following the example of her older brother, "is that he never pampered me with girl gifts such as dolls, dresses, make-up and jewelry. He gifted me with things that enhanced my education and for expanding my horizons. When I began to work as a sales lady in a milliner store he encouraged me to think about being promoted to supervisor, then to personnel director, then to manager and finally, owning my own store. His generous business loan made that happen."

"Uncle Ebenezer demonstrated abundant pride in my accomplishments by attending the opening of each of my stores. This gesture spoke volumes about his moral support. In addition, he made helpful suggestions about stocking special items for men that would draw them in as new customers. He often challenged me with his business-inspired wisdom: 'Martha, think like a customer.' It took me awhile to catch his meaning, but after I did he didn't need to repeat it."

Thinking less is more, Martha pared down her original eulogy with these words.

"I stand here today as testimony to a respected business man and philanthropist who mentored me into a business woman. I am who I am because he helped me to see who I could become with his eyes, his vision, his kindness, his generosity and most of all, his stubbornness in never letting me give up on my gifts and dreams."

She paused, deciding to end on a humorous note.

"When I used the word, *stubborn* with him he winked and said, "Stubborn was the old me. Fortitude, Martha, is the new me."

As she returned to the pew, her youngest brother, Tim, took her place.

The mourners who filled the church were familiar with the special relationship that Tim Cratchit had forged with Ebenezer Scrooge. Their history spanned sixteen years. At the time of their first meeting, the close circle of the Cratchit friends knew the soft-spoken boy as 'Tiny Tim.'

He had been afflicted throughout his young life with various illnesses and physical handicaps that kept him confined at home for endless periods of time, and prevented him from engaging in sporting events with his friends. His conditions, at times, grew to be so grave that Alice devoted herself as mother, nurse and teacher, schooling him at home to both cheer his spirits and to make sure he was not deprived of a quality education.

While Alice taught him the basics in reading, writing, literature and science, she deferred to Bob to instruct him in arithmetic. This one-to-one ratio of teacher to student would serve Tim well when it came time to choosing a career.

When Mr. Scrooge made his memorable visit to the Cratchit's home on the first Christmas Eve following his mysterious conversion, he paid special attention to Tiny Tim. Following that visit Bob confided to Tim that he met with Scrooge privately.

"Bob," he said, "put down your ledger as I wish to discuss a proposal for having Tim evaluated by medical specialists at the premiere teaching hospital here in London."

"My dad was totally surprised. Uncle Scrooge used dad's speechlessness to brook no argument about paying those bills, and was present for every examination, every test, every surgery and every recovery."

Thus began a friendship with Tiny Tim that left Ebenezer Scrooge feeling as if he had gained an adopted son. Just as much, Tim had gained an adopted uncle.

"He did not confine his surprises to my dad only. One day he visited my mother. Alice, he said, I would like to relieve you of some of your duties in raising the children by having tutors to help keep Tim abreast of his school work."

"He anticipated my mother's argument, and put her at ease with the assurance that he would pay the expense. Uncle Scrooge kept those tutors on his payroll for two years."

By the time Tim was fifteen, his health had improved significantly. He returned to school and graduated from the secondary level with honors. During this time his medical treatments included a diet of regular exercise, which eventually turned him into a respectable cricket player. In addition, one of his tutors, Reginald Iverson, taught Tim to master the game of chess. In time, the budding adolescent taught his Uncle Scrooge. From then on, the two became passionate competitive players.

When it came time for Tim to choose a career, no one was surprised when he announced his desire to attend medical school. Nor was any Cratchit surprised when Uncle Ebenezer insisted on paying the bills.

Standing next to the casket of his devoted adopted uncle, Tim Cratchit was a spitting image of his father and every bit a respectable medical professional. His parents were proud of all their children, but Tim held a special place in their hearts. Unlike his two siblings, Tim had far more hurdles to sprint in childhood. A spinal deformity at birth complicated his mobility during his early growth process, and occasional bouts of colic and borderline pneumonia kept him bedridden much of his early childhood years.

Tim never allowed these burdens to weaken his spirit or cloud his morale. Nor did he ever morph into a complainer. Bitterness did not become him. Rather, through the years of balancing physical ailments with spiritual growth, he developed a character unlike his brother and sister. He had no choice but to grow inner wells of hope and courage that kept him focused on embracing life with a determination to find meaning in it, no matter the crosses he carried.

It was this childlike inner fortitude that Ebenezer Scrooge noticed in Tim, a kind of inner glow Tim emitted as expressive of the way he carried himself. Little did the budding adolescent realize that his calm behavior awakened a new desire in the transformed Scrooge to have some of that inner glow for himself?

Scrooge carried a deep desire to catch some of Tim's unique temperament. This new desire confirmed Scrooge's conversion – he was encountering people and things with new inner eyes.

"Before his passing, Scrooge shared a vulnerable moment with my dad. He courageously shared with him that I was the only person he knew that lived a truly harmonic life. He expressed it this way to my father."

"Bob, I am captivated by Tim appearing to be the same on the inside as well as on the outside. My dad was lost for words." Upon hearing those words, father and son shared an endearing moment, wearing similar smiles.

Mr. Scrooge went on to say, "Tim has an inner glow from the victories over his sufferings that I lack but noticing it makes my heart grow fonder for him."

Many of those in the congregation agreed with Tim's sentiments. Thus, they appreciated his vulnerability as truly authentic. He was an original and not a typecast. Due to his journey from being a sick child to acquiring the noble title of physician, everyone's respect for Tim was rooted in his constitution. It was no trivial feat to turn his years of sickness and suffering into a career of caring for others. Everyone harbored their own sentiments that medicine was more than a profession. It was Tim's vocation, his calling to give back some of the love and care bestowed on him during his uncertain childhood years.

"Good Morning. I am Tim Cratchit," he said clearly, but in the trademark soft spoken voice of his family. Introducing himself, without the title 'Doctor" enhanced his credibility with the assembly. If their smiles could speak they would say, "thank you for still being one of us."

"Like my siblings, I too claim Mr. Scrooge as an adopted uncle. That honor goes back many years to the days when he, like many of you, was a care giver to an anxious little boy who suffered through too many years of ill health."

He paused to recognize the faces of those who were his childhood cheer-leaders when he needed support as a child.

"Now that little boy is a doctor giving back to many of you, neighbors and friends, some of the care and cheer you gave to me when I needed it. That includes Uncle Scrooge. I owe my career and many other blessings to him. I had the pleasure the past two years of being his personal physician. He never complained about my bedside manners or prescriptions, though he occasionally grumbled about the attention, arguing that people far more sick that he needed my time and care."

Tim paused turning it into a reverent moment.

"When he turned sixty-eight, he insisted I let him age gracefully. When I asked him what he meant by that, he said, "Let's make your visits occasions for dinner, conversation and good port, rather than only to check my pulse and heartbeat. Your company would be far more enjoyable than just having you show up with a stethoscope and ask me to say 'aah.'"

Tim maintained eye contact while continuing, "It was his way of subtly suggesting that together we will have one less regret in life if we drink enough good wine."

"I acquiesced because I caught his meaning. But, also because I had grown a fondness for his port."

The chuckles throughout the congregation evoked a smile on Tim's youthful and cherubic face.

"Something told me that what he was hinting at would impact my profession as a physician. So I welcomed our visits like looking through a pair of glasses. One lens helped me to treasure our special friendship and reminisce about the memories we had that glued us together as endearing friends. Through the other lens I saw him as a unique patient who would teach me valuable lessons about how to help people in advanced age to grow old gracefully. Through that lens I saw his house as a laboratory with Uncle Scrooge as my mentor."

"So those of you here today who are ready to age gracefully, I am ready to share with you some of the lessons I learned from Uncle Scrooge, though I must add without the port!"

The congregation had taken to Tim as a storyteller as much as many of them had valued him as their physician.

"On behalf of my wife, Julianne, and our two children, I am honored to have eulogized Uncle Ebenezer today. He wanted to be remembered not for the good he did with his wealth, but by how sharing the wealth of his new heart and spirit enabled him to be remembered as a changed man, whose goodness inspired people to be good to others. As he would frequently say, 'that is how to keep the spirit of Christmas all year through.'"

"May that be said of all of us one day as we take to heart the stories we have heard of the life of one changed man – a man who changed the lives of so many others."

His closing words echoed through the church like an epitaph for an unconventional requiem.

"He insisted I close as follows, 'God bless us, everyone.'"

The congregation took its cue from the choir and stood in unison to sing all verses of Amazing Grace, with full organ accompaniment. Scrooge had instructed the Vicar to limit his preaching to a few minutes, implying that God needed to be glorified equally with prayers and hymns as much as Scrooge was embarrassingly gloried through eulogies. The Vicar was not amused, but complied fearing that Scrooge's wealth might have enough influence in the afterlife to return and haunt the Vicar.

Once the funeral ended, Fred, his family, and the Cratchits were ushered down the aisle. In the narthex they proudly stood in line greeting the mourners as they exited the iconic church.

"I was truly inspired by your words," said the editor of the London Daily News to Fred Cratchit. "You made me proud to know your uncle."

"Thank you Martha," said one of her most ardent customers. "Your testimony lifted the hopes and spirits of every woman in the congregation."

Shaking the hand of Bob Cratchit firmly, a loyal client commented, "The firm of Scrooge and Cratchit is in good hands. I look forward to investing in Mr. Scrooge's legacy with you."

Once the church emptied, these two families, Scrooge's house staff and a few close colleagues waited for the funeral carriage to arrive. After the body of Scrooge was placed inside, they formed a procession of carriages to the parish cemetery several blocks away for a private internment.

The final ritual was vintage Ebenezer Scrooge. He disliked the morbid tradition of mourners throwing a hand-full of dirt on a coffin in a grave. Instead, he instructed Fred to bring a carafe of his favorite vintage port and wine glasses to toast his passing with flair while licking their lips in sweet delight reminiscent of sweet memories of him.

No one knew that this idea of a final departure was born from Scrooge's converted imagination, the one that encountered the three spirits of Christmas past, present and future that visited him that magical Christmas Eve. The dreaded spirit of Christmas yet-to-come had put the final seal of conversion on Scrooge's heart. It changed him so profoundly that he reversed the curse of Christmas-of- things-yet-to-come by allowing all three spirits to radically change him.

His new life story came to a close the way he re-scripted the story of Scrooge the miser to a story of Scrooge the good uncle, good friend, good neighbor, and good benefactor. The reformed Scrooge had the last words. While raising his glass in the gesture of a toast, Fred, uttered one of his uncle's famous lines from Elizabeth Barrett Browning:

> *"What I do and what I dream include Thee, as wine must taste of its own grapes."*

The families in attendance raised their glasses and in unison, responded, "Here, here." Only Mrs. Dilber, Mr. Scrooge's devoted housekeeper, let her tears flow while Alice Cratchit held her hand gently as a gesture of comfort. With unhurried enthusiasm, the port was pleasantly savored until the last drop.

Scrooge bequeathed his three-story Mayfair townhouse to Fred, and he had placed a substantial sum of money in escrow for Mrs. Dilber's salary. She would remain as the housekeeper for the next five years adding joy to her life as she learned to sing the songs of Fred and Catherine's three children. Their young and boisterous voices echoed through the house, adding color and cheer in every room that had been neatly redecorated by Catherine.

After Scrooge's passing, plentiful spirits of joy and merriment wafted through the house each and every Christmas season. It was contagious to all who visited during the holidays and was plentiful enough to spread and share with others throughout the New Year.

CHAPTER 2

Bob Cratchit

*B*ob Cratchit acquired his accounting skills naturally. While growing up, he had the good fortune of being blessed with parents who valued education. His father was the manager of a West Indies shipping company with docking piers in east London. His mother was a sales lady at a local haberdashery. From her he learned more about arithmetic than he did in school. From his father he learned business skills that would serve him well later in life.

Bob's younger sibling died in early childhood from scarlet fever, leaving Bob with parents whose grief quickly turned to a double portion of lavish love and attention for their surviving child. Consequently, Bob grew up knowing he was loved and how to share love. He vowed early that whenever he married, Bob and his wife would have enough children to spare them from just one child with no siblings.

His parents were deeply religious, passing on a strong and reverent faith to their son. Raised to respect the formal and somewhat stern traditions of the Anglican Church, he was also deeply loyal to Queen Victoria as head of the Church of England. Such loyalty would be later easily translated into his work ethics as an accounting clerk. His firm sense of perseverance would reap employment dividends, first as an underpaid employee to a miserly accountant, and, later as a business partner with the miser, turned-into a kind-hearted employer.

As Bob Cratchit grew his skills for managing personal loans and ledgers, he also developed a genuinely humble and highly tolerant character. During interviews these virtues assured future employers, that he was a dependable, honest and trustworthy employee. Far from pursuing work just to be a reliable breadwinner for his family, it mattered equally to Bob that his reputation be esteemed by his bosses and that he fulfill his vocation as unselfish husband and father of a family.

When he first hired his new bookkeeper, Ebenezer Scrooge had little character himself, so he wasn't particularly interested in that quality in an employee. In his mind, he was simply hiring a clerk the day Bob Cratchit arrived for an interview. It was June 28, 1835 at the office of Scrooge & Marley. Bob had not heard glowing things about the two businessmen, but the recent birth of his second child took precedence over being too selective about a job. He arrived ten minutes early and to his surprise found their office closed. He wondered if he should leave a hand-written message. Not wanting to appear disingenuous, he decided to wait on the stoop by the front door.

The two business partners arrived thirty minutes late, appearing almost oblivious to his presence and equally unapologetic for their disregard for promptness. They made him wait another twenty minutes in the outer office while they reviewed the details of a business acquisition made earlier that morning.

Through this humiliation, Bob Cratchit remained steady and calm. Finally, Jacob Marley, the older of the two partners, opened a glass-framed door and invited Bob into the inner office.

Scrooge and Marley both sat behind their desks, assuming an attitude of two vultures overlooking prey with their hands folded. Mr. Marley, twitching his fingers, somewhat nervously, broke the ice.

"Tell us about your education and specifically, your facility with bookkeeping."

Assuming a calm posture and in a steady voice, Bob obliged.

"My parents schooled me at an early age. My father is a business man with a shipping company in east London and my mother is a cashier at a haberdashery. My mother taught me the basics of arithmetic. My father taught me the skill of balancing books and how to live within a budget."

He decided less was more so he thought those words were sufficient.

Mr. Scrooge was more probing in his questions and brusque in his tone.

"How old are you?

"Thirty-five, sir"

"Are you married?"

"Yes, sir,"

"Do you have children?"

"Yes sir, a boy and a girl."

"Do you have any references?"

"Yes sir, I work part time at Guilford's Mercantile and at St. Giles Church."

"Do either of those positions have anything to do with accounting?"

"Yes sir!"

"The position here is fulltime, eight hours a day. Weekends are free. We don't pay for working on national holidays."

Bob shook his head in agreement thinking it best to remain silent.

"The salary is sixteen shillings a week. When can you begin?"

"The first of next week sir," Bob said decidedly.

"We can have a working contract ready to be signed and witnessed then. Is this agreed?"

Bob and Jacob Marley shook their heads in unison.

Both men extended their hands in a gentlemanly fashion. Mr. Scrooge ended the twenty-minute interview in a taciturn fashion.

"See you on Monday. And be prompt."

Bob thought that last line was condescending considering they were thirty minutes late for his interview. Nevertheless, his generous nature led him to brush it off and leave with a wide smile.

Once Bob exited the office, he was suddenly aware of misgivings, which he quickly suppressed by the thought that a permanent job would go a long way in feeding a family of four. He reluctantly concluded that the meager salary they offered could be augmented by keeping his weekend janitorial job at St. Giles Church.

He began scripting how he would share this good news with Mrs. Cratchit, minus his misgivings about the unctuous and seemingly sinister Mr. Scrooge. Bob caught his judgments quickly, and just as quickly forgave himself. He had every intention of beginning this new position with a heart free of intimidations and misjudgments. He believed his kind and gentle nature could assuage any opponent and leaned on that conviction resolving that this new job would pay ample dividends for his family and his new employer.

With barely a foot in the door, Alice Cratchit began peppering him with questions.

"I have the kettle on for some tea. While it's boiling tell me all about your interview." Alice Cratchit was her husband's first and best cheerleader.

Bob decided to jump right to the good news.

"Well, my dear, I must have impressed them because I was offered the full-time position and I begin work on Monday."

"That's wonderful news! I had no doubt that you would impress them, my dear. But were you impressed with them?"

Bob maintained his composure. He remained philosophical in his reply.

"Well my dear, it was more important to impress them today. My impressions of them will come later. Don't you agree?"

Alice Cratchit continually saw herself as a partner in their marriage. Her genuine interest overcame any inclination to be submissive to her husband.

""What salary did they offer? That will speak volumes about first impressions."

Clearing his throat, Bob spoke in a pensive tone.

"Sixteen shillings a week, my dear."

Horrified, Alice retorted:

"Was that negotiable?"

"Well, my dear, I thought it best to accept their offer rather than irritate them. I am sure in time I will receive promotions and a salary increase."

"Did you request that those points be written into your contract?"

"My dear, I trust them to reward my skills and worthiness in due time."

"With four mouths to feed I hope those rewards come quickly."

Alice made her point, but not as delicately as Bob had wished. His comeback was intended to convey assurance.

"With the six additional shillings from St. Giles, we should feel blessed right now. God will not abandon us, my dear."

Alice frowned and curled her eyes while serving tea and biscuits. The children were doing school work upstairs. Father and mother enjoyed the quiet while sipping their favorite beverage. These afternoon delights would end on Monday, so they relished this time together like a holy hour.

On Saturday, Alice washed and ironed dress shirts for Bob to wear for the coming week. She was determined that her husband look entirely worthy of his new job.

On Sunday, the family attended the 11:00 am service at St. Giles. Alice and Bob both prayed that this position as a clerk would open new doors for him that would eventually benefit the family.

Little did either of them know that God was listening, but would test the mettle of Bob's patience for the next ten years.

As agreed, Bob arrived at the firm of Scrooge and Marley on Monday at 8:55 am. To his surprise both businessmen were in their office hard at work. While Scrooge's eyes deflected to the miniature pendulum clock on the wall, Marley never took his eyes off a ledger. Though the door to their inner office was closed, Bob clearly saw them ignore him through the glass panes. Bob, waiting for one of them to greet him and give him some instructions about his first work day, stood in his small workspace for nearly thirty minutes before Ebenezer Scrooge acknowledged his presence. He delivered instructions in a cold and calculated voice. Nonetheless, Bob demurred with a well-crafted smile and the assurance that the instructions were clear.

After six months, Scrooge and Marley evaluated Bob's performance. Neither of the ominous businessmen was endowed with the gift of flattery. When they informed him that he would continue working as their clerk, he expected the surprise of a small salary increase. But it was Bob who was surprised when that benefit was not mentioned. He withheld that sadness from his wife, thinking it better for their marital bliss.

The routine of working as a clerk for Scrooge and Marley was not a pleasant one. His employers, while not openly hostile toward him, were painfully indifferent. They were far more educated and wealthy than Bob, but their temperaments were devoid of good manners and good will. They were absorbed with making money and cared little for who they hurt or alienated in acquiring it. In time, Bob learned to remain silent when his employers sent clients in arrears on their loans, to work houses until the debts were paid. While his tongue was tied, Bob's heart bled with compassion for the families of those debtors.

One particular client seared his heart. Alistair Ferguson owed the firm fifty Pounds plus interest. He was three months in arrears the day he was summoned to the office. Five minutes after Bob announced him to Scrooge and Marley, a constable arrived. The penny-pinching misers had pre-arranged a possible arrest.

"You are three months delinquent in repaying your loan. Either make a payment today, or the constable in the clerk's office will escort you to prison." Scrooge spoke with no mercy in his voice to the shaking client.

Mr. Ferguson pleaded with him.

"I need more time, sir, please."

"Did we ask for more time in deciding to give you a loan?" Marley retorted.

"Either make a payment today or go to jail," Scrooge said condescendingly.

"Sir, please, I have a wife and four children at home."

"That is no concern of ours," Scrooge bellowed.

Devoid of any pity, Marley instructed the constable to escort the debtor to prison. As they exited, Bob's heart ached.

One month later, Bob and his eldest old son, Peter secretly visited Alistair Ferguson at the Marshalsea Prison, surprising him with a box of figs and nuts and fresh flowers, a touching tribute from Alice Cratchit. Watching his father practice this work of mercy left a lasting impression on Peter. Fully realizing how much happiness and fulfillment Bob experienced in giving selflessly and not receiving, Peter vowed to grow his own heart through this kind of charity, as a special way to honor his father. By the end of his first year at the accounting firm, he and his son were visiting as many as a half-dozen clients at the Marshalsea. During that time they became friends with spouses, children and other Good Samaritans of the prisoners.

When they returned home, Bob was often reluctant to discuss their visits with the debtors. Peter, however, couldn't contain himself and shared details. As Alice listened, she swelled with pride for her husband and the wondrous example he was setting for their son. She knew this form of personal witness was better for his religious formation than any catechism lesson Peter studied at St. Giles.

On the first Christmas Eve at Scrooge & Marley, Bob expected to be excused early, handed a bonus and dismissed with the greeting "Merry Christmas!" Those expectations quickly soured when two advocates from the children's workhouse entered the office seeking a donation. Marley had departed early. Scrooge told them Christmas was a "Bah Humbug," and that he was not inclined to dispense charity on one particular day of the year. "Are there not work-houses, are there no prisons?" he retorted. They were escorted from the office empty-handed.

At 6:00 pm Scrooge growled at Bob.

"I suppose you will want all day off tomorrow."

"If it's convenient, sir," Bob replied timidly.

"It's not convenient….but be here all the earlier the day after."

"Thank you, Sir and, Merry Christmas."

Bob realized his mistake when Scrooge's eyes tightened at the sound of those words. He quickly wrapped his scarf twice around his neck, grabbed his gloves, extinguished the tallow candle atop his desk and left the office dancing with merriment in his steps. It was intended as a rebuke to Scrooge's miserly temperament.

On the way home he picked up his wife's Christmas gift at a local jeweler and made the final payment. He mused about how she would fuss about the expensive brooch, deflecting her attention away from asking about a Christmas bonus. If this plan backfired, Bob was prepared with the closest thing to a legitimate excuse. To be safe, however, he implored both God and Santa to spare him that option.

CHAPTER 3

*A*lice Cratchit exhibited her own accounting skills in managing the family household. She was frugal, but not cheap. The children came first with both parents carefully discerning the difference between their needs from their wants.

However, at Christmas no expense was spared for merriment and feasting. Each year, Bob somehow managed a small turkey for Christmas dinner. Alice planned ahead for chestnut stuffing, yams, baked bread and plum pudding. On Christmas Day this poor family was abundantly rich in love and faith and goodness toward those who were poorer.

They traditionally attended the Christmas Eve service at St. Giles. This enabled them to put God first. On Christmas Day they decorated their modest house, while singing carols, offering prayers of thanksgiving and sharing Christmas stockings filled with startling gifts. While dinner was cooking, Bob and Peter visited the Marshalsea and shared Christmas cookies with the prisoners, who by now, they call friends. Peter found joy in reading the Nativity story, ending it in his own words.

"The birth of the Christ child, in a lowly stable, among animals and poor shepherds, is meant to remind all of you how special you are to God. You may be in debt to other fellow humans, but this holy feast reminds us that we are all indebted to God for raising our dignity with the birth of his only son. My father and I are honored to share such dignity with you on this happy day."

Peter's words so easily brought tears to Bob's eyes, and to all those prisoners who felt loved through his sentiments.

The following year on Christmas Eve, Jacob Marley died. When the housekeeper delivered the news, Scrooge left the office. He returned an hour later and simply resumed his work. Bob concluded that the rare grin on his face was due, no doubt, to a double portion of income that Scrooge expected to pocket with Marley's death.

When Bob and Alice paid their respects at the funeral at Lothrop Morticians two days later, they were shocked that only ten people attended. Scrooge arrived late and departed early, but not before sternly reminding Bob to return to the office and resume work within thirty minutes.

"Work doesn't cease when people die. Be quick about your farewell; dismiss your grief and return to work quickly. I am not paying you to mourn."

Bob signaled with a slight bow of his head, but Alice was tempted to kick Scrooge in the shin. She wasted no respect on him and just as quickly thought it best not to waste any adverse energy on him, either.

The following year at Christmas Alice was with child. Unlike Peter and Martha, this third child was problematic. Alice's motherly instinct convinced her early that something was wrong. The child in her womb was restless. She was overly nauseous, experiencing troublesome and interminable bouts of irritation and worry.

Bob and the children tried to comfort her as much as possible. But Christmas that year was not the same with her shifting moods, distress and elevated levels of delirium. During the last month of her pregnancy, Bob was forced to hire a nurse to care for Alice at home. As soon as she gave birth in mid-January, their newborn son, Tim, was whisked off to the hospital and placed in a children's ward. Alice's delicate health required home nursing care for a month. Only after another month would she would be strong enough to hold him in her arms. The doctors told Bob and Alice that their newborn had a deformed spine and would not live long. This devastating news tore at their heartstrings.

They quickly stormed heaven with prayers asking the infant Christ child to intercede. Their anxieties were private, but their hope was shared in union of prayer.

"Lord God, the birth of your son took place under unusual circumstances. But you looked after him and guided his life from childhood to adulthood. We ask the same for our new born son, Tim. Be a healing presence in his handicaps. Our faith is strong that you have some special purpose for him as you did for your son, Jesus. May Tim grow up to fulfill his mission so he can join your son, Jesus in giving you glory. Amen."

Each morning and evening, Bob and Alice lit a candle, bowed their heads reverently and held hands while uttering this prayer. Close by, Peter and Martha whispered their own.

Adding to Bob's stress was the vexing issue of how to pay for the hospital bill. It was an unexpected item he did not factor into the household budget. Seeing no way out of this emergency, he gave in to his worst fears and approached Mr. Scrooge for a loan. He leaned on his credibility and trustworthiness as an employee, hoping to assuage his miserly boss and appeal to whatever ounce of compassion he secretly possessed. He waited until the end of the work day to meet with his temperamental boss, thinking he might need to stop by a pub for a calming pint of beer before proceeding home.

"Mr. Scrooge may I have a few moments of your time, please?" His voice was steady and his stature was calm."

"What for?" Scrooge grumbled without any eye contact.

"I have a personal matter to discuss."

"Make it quick, it is nearly closing time," Scrooge retorted without taking his eyes off the ledger on his desk.

"Well, sir, my newest child, Tim, was born with severe health issues, and was hospitalized for a month. He is now home with us, but I am worried about paying the hospital bills. I need to ask if you can advance me a loan of twenty Pounds."

"What is your plan for repaying it?" Scrooge paid no deference to his faithful clerk as he continued to focus on calculating figures.

"I would ask, sir that you withhold one shilling a week from my salary until the loan is repaid."

The stingy business man scribbled some figures on a piece of paper. Then, to Bob's bewilderment, responded,

"At one percent interest, that would take you nearly two years to repay."

Bob's quick emotional recovery enabled him to craft a reply that would, hopefully, please his boss.

"That is agreeable to me, sir. If you would be so kind as to draft a loan agreement I would be happy to sign it." As Scrooge handed Bob a ledger sheet, he snapped,

"We will attend to that in the morning. Enter these figures in the current loan ledger...........and be quick to finish before you leave for the day."

Bob remained in the office fifteen extra minutes before departing for home. On his way he treated himself to a pint at Copperfield's Pub. He needed to replenish the energy output he expended in his tense encounter with Scrooge.

The first gulp of the tasty Irish brew began to calm the resentment he felt realizing that his boss never inquired about the health of his new son. A second gulp eased his ill-humor with Scrooge's entire lack of interest in the state of Alice's health. A third gulp calmed his frazzled emotions knowing he would not share with his wife the loan agreement he just made. Bob would spare her the unnecessary stress of spiraling into apoplexy. He didn't need to compound her current condition with such news.

Bob vowed to find some way to compensate for the loss of that weekly shilling, even if it meant working extra hours as a street sweeper. When it came to supporting his family, parenting took precedence over pride.

The final gulp of his brew was a promise to himself. He half-raised the glass: "I will not let the stinginess of my boss infect my heart. One of him is enough. I raise my glass to my virtue of charity and will forever be merciful to him. One day God will repay me with surprising dividends."

As he emptied the tankard, he licked his lips while musing to himself:

"To make sure you heard that plea, O God, let me add, 'Amen.'"

In time, the family prayers for Tiny Tim did not fall on deaf ears. Eventually, Tim achieved a minimal quality of life in spite of his spinal abnormalities. For the first seven years of his life, he wobbled around using a home-made crutch. Instead of pampering him, his father insisted he exercise daily, and the two of them were often seen walking in Camden Town Park.

Whenever Tim tired during the walks Bob would hoist him on his shoulder and carry him. This scene reminded neighbors of the biblical image of a shepherd carrying a sheep.

Bob never showed the slightest embarrassment about his son's physical condition. Far from adopting the usual attitude of treating such a child as a curse, the Cratchit's lavished great love and care on Tim. It was the energy he needed to transcend his condition and live life as normally and fully as possible.

On his best days Tim attended school with his neighbors. On his worst days, Alice tutored him, while leaving the subject of arithmetic to her mathematically advanced husband. They never discussed that Tim should be treated differently from the other children.

"Look at my test score in arithmetic," Tim would proudly shout waving the test paper in front of his father the very minute he returned home from work.

"You earned that 'A' Tim," Bob delighted to say. It widened the boy's smile until his adoring father mirrored it back to him.

In spite of their misfortunes, the happiest time of the year for the Cratchit family was Christmas. Poor as church mice, with singular devotion and contagious cheer, Bob inspired his meager family to make merry every Christmas as if they were royalty living in St. James Palace. The devoted husband and father never allowed economics to frustrate his imagination.

For ten long years he endured the humiliation of working for Scrooge without any substantial pay raise suffering through ten Christmas seasons without a bonus. He quietly endured repaying a loan, at one percent interest. For ten years he deleted the voice of "Bah Humbug" from his mind and resisted thinking the worst of Mr. Scrooge's vapid attitude toward Christmas.

He did all that for his family. His humility and self-deprecating manner were the best gifts he could give them for Christmas. It was the humble Christ child's most endearing gift to the human family and it was bestowed on Bob Cratchit abundantly. The cherished husband and father made God look good by the way he revealed and shared that piece of the divine in him with others.

In spite of Ebenezer Scrooge's best efforts, no one was ever able to steal Christmas from the Cratchit family. Bob's predisposition for happiness was typically much stronger than Scrooge's strain for misery. Christmas merriment, like his love and fidelity toward his family, flowed throughout Bob Cratchit's blood. For him, they went together, like singing and feasting on the honored day that was complemented with decorating their house, trimming a tree, stuffing stockings, writing cards, roasting turkey, and enjoying the Brandy-laced flavor of Alice's seasonal plum pudding.

The Christmas cheer and merriment that the Cratchit's spread among the community in Camden Town was equally infectious. Those who could afford it surprised their poorer neighbors with gifts anonymously left at their doors. Along the streets, families exchanged cookies and small fruit cakes as freely as they shared, "Merry Christmas." No "Humbugs" lived in their neighborhood. They were converted by, an abundance of caroling, decorating, and of spreading enough merriment to last a whole year. It was their way of putting a communal face on the mystery of God becoming one of them.

On Christmas Day every adult in Camden Town was a child spreading the happiness and delight of what it was like for God to get out of the heavens and appear on earth as a cooing, happy, vulnerable child.

However, on Christmas Day 1850, a miracle came upon this blessed family. It affected them profoundly and wondrously altered the course of their lives. It gave new credence to the power of prayer and revitalized their belief that even the worst of human beings can awaken in the hearts of other stubborn and selfish people the desire to live life for the purpose of making a difference.

On that Christmas Day, a twenty pound turkey surprisingly arrived at their door. Attached to the legs of the giant bird was a simple postal card bearing a hand-written message: "Merry Christmas to the Cratchit Family."

The absence of the giver's name created five confused faces. Tiny Tim guessed it was from Mr. Scrooge. Four confused faces were speechless. It didn't take long for Alice to trim, and stuff and cook this bountiful gift.

When Bob arrived for work the following day Scrooge shocked him with unexpected news - he was increasing Bob's salary, including accrued interest over the past ten years.

While offering Bob a glass of his finest brandy, Scrooge confessed to sending the turkey on Christmas Day. His typical scowling face had unexpectedly been replaced by one beaming with happiness.

In a cheerful tone, to complement his altered disposition, Scrooge declared thoughtfully, "I haven't lost my senses, Bob. I have come to them. I am sorry for the years of misery I have put you through and my negative attitude that discarded your kindness. All of that changes today along with a promise to be more caring toward your family, especially Tiny Tim."

Bob's frozen emotions gradually thawed.

"I am most grateful Mr. Scrooge for your change of heart."

Scrooge had the final word, which delighted Bob immensely.

"Why don't you go out and buy some more coal to warm up the offices?"

The life of a stunned clerk and the lives of his wife and children were forever changed by a miracle and a mystery that Bob experienced deeply, but could not explain. Without hesitation, every Christmas afterwards, Bob savored his blessings with a double portion of gratitude.

The conversion of Ebenezer Scrooge that Christmas Eve forever re-scripted the story of the Cratchit family, who, in turn, altered the lives of many others. Conversion and charity wove threads of hope in each of them from that day forward and left a trail of light and goodness for others to follow.

CHAPTER 4

Alice Cratchit

Alice Cratchit was born into a poor family, but amply compensated with the good fortune of being a fiercely independent woman. Her father died in an industrial accident when she was five, leaving her mother to care for her and a younger brother. They moved into a modest house with her Aunt Josephine, her mother's older, strong-willed and eccentric sister. 'Aunt Joe,' as she was affectionately called, had an amiable disposition and a rallying imagination. She quickly recognized the independent streak in Alice and encouraged her to develop it, as she put it, "as a survival skill in male-dominated England."

When Alice's mother reprimanded Martha for getting into fights with boys at school, Aunt Joe would affirm her. While her mother was a disciplinarian, her endearing Aunt was a personal coach, guiding her in the values of free-lance thinking and behaviors that she knew were indispensable to a strong-willed woman.

Unfortunately, Theodore, Alice's younger brother, bore the wrath of his sister's indentured pride. Three years her junior, Teddy, was frustrated from acquiring his own sense of personal freedom by Alice's urges to control and tease him. When he turned sixteen, Teddy ran away from home and hired himself out as a worker on a cargo ship. After traveling the world he returned ten years later with a small fortune and an attractive wife from the West Indies. He reconciled with his ill-mother and Aunt, but not with his sister. Unfortunately, the scars of her youthful behaviors to shame and control him had not healed. Alice's obstinate attitudes toward Teddy in his childhood turned him into a man resentful of his sister. They remained strangers the rest of their lives.

This adversity with her only sibling left Alice with deep emotional scars. In late adolescence she acquired a skill as an expert seamstress, though she plied her trade with the contemplativeness of a cloistered nun. This was the self-inflicted penance for fueling the estrangement from her brother.

Every stitch she sewed was a form of repairing the damaged relationship with her only sibling. With every finished dress or laced blouse, she felt more complete as a human, humble person. As she cut cloth she cut away a little more of the old Alice. A new Alice was imprinted on each new article of clothing.

One day, in her mid-twenties, Alice Clifton attended Saturday Vespers at St. Giles Church, after which she was approached by a handsome, soft-spoken gentleman who introduced himself as Bob Cratchit.

"Do you attend St. Giles regularly?" he asked with shyness in his voice.

Appreciating the warm nature of his assertiveness, the converted Alice engaged him in an equally warm manner.

"Not as regularly as I should."

His next line took her completely by surprise.

"In that case, may I invite you to join me for services tomorrow morning and afterwards for a stroll in Camden Town Park?"

Alice repaid his surprise.

"I happily accept your offer. My name is Alice Clifton."

The pleasant expression on his face equaled the pleasant feelings stirring inside her. She decided to keep those hidden for now. Ten years of living as a spinster had grown her emotions to a cautionary stage in adulthood. She was not being mischievous, but rather protective of alienating a stranger the way she had estranged her own brother. Alice was willing to trust the warmth of a young Bob Cratchit to discover how a trusting heart opens doors to new friendships, and eventually, to the magic and mystery of love. She had missed both for too many years.

They met again in the church narthex on Sunday morning. Bob was impressed with her apparel. The blouse and skirt were exquisitely stitched and fit her as if they were tailored. It left him wondering if Alice was a woman of independent means.

After the service, they strolled in the park talking like strangers slowly edging each other's hearts toward friendship. Alice shared details about her naturally acquired tailoring skills.

"It wasn't anything I had planned. One day I saw a sewing machine in an appliance store and was fascinated by the saleslady operating it. A voice told me I can do that. The next thing I knew, I was tailoring clothes."

She paused before adding: "In time it became my profession." Although it filled her mind, she omitted the chapter and verse about stitching and sewing clothes being a spiritual metaphor as penance for the irreparable rips and tears she had made in the relationship with her brother.

Bob reciprocated with details about his life.

"My parents are kind and hard-working people. I look forward to your meeting them someday. Perhaps we can plan a Sunday dinner with them in the future."

Alice liked the gentle cadence of Bob's voice and respected his pauses as something quite natural for him.

"I had a younger brother, Everett, who died quite young of scarlet fever. My parents' grief turned into lavish love for me. While I feel blessed by their affection, I continued a longing for another sibling."

Alice felt moved by his vulnerability and took it into her heart as a quality of strength she came to admire in him. It was a kind of strength she wished she had shown with her brother, Teddy. Bob continued the dialogue.

"My parents' skills in accounting and business inspired me to develop an interest in finance, which in turn helped me to secure a job in the business office at Guilford's Department Store."

The more he talked about his job, the more Alice respected him. Far from sounding haughty she savored the manner in which he spoke about his hopes for marriage and raising a family. It sounded inclusive of her own desires for a spouse, and for intimacy with a man, intimacy that had been absent from her life far too long. Bob's delicate style found a welcome place in her heart. She let it rest there hoping that it would grow into a longing for Bob Cratchit to be that special man.

As they approached the pond Bob bought a bag of peanuts from a vendor. They sat on a bench, cracked the shells and teased the geese to come closer for feeding. Strangely, their bantering of the geese was a form of romantically teasing each other, a desire they both felt on the inside. The allure of that emotion only fueled the humorous ways they tormented the quacking creatures. They both relished the fun of the moment and savored it as a lasting memory of their stroll.

"I've walked the park many times, but never teased the geese like this," Alice commented.

"I do it all the time," Bob replied. "It helps to improve my playful and creative skills with people." He let his innuendo hang in the air like the breeze that was swaying between the trees. Alice decoded his meaning and cracked an approving smile.

As they exited the park, Bob asked if she would join him for dinner on Friday evening. She gladly accepted. They went their separate ways but not before honoring the etiquette of a gentlemanly bow and a modest curtsy.

When Alice returned home she replayed the events of the day as pictures floating through her memory. She retrieved Bob's words as if she were recalling lines from her favorite Jane Austen novels. His soft spoken demeanor was nothing like the insufferable pride of Edward D'Arcy in *Pride and Prejudice*. His gentle manner was distinctly different from the rough edges of Colonel Brandon in *Sense and Sensibility*. Bob's manner was more soft-edged and so gracefully laced with a tinge of humor.

Alice Clifton spent the rest of that Sunday crafting Bob Cratchit as the main figure in the next chapter of her life story. If she was lucky, he would join her in writing those remaining chapters and verses as husband and wife.

As her imagination awakened, she accepted the fact that Bob wasn't a dashing landowner. But Alice was not looking for that noble man. Neither was he a humble vicar with a vetted parish in his future. Nor was he a highly successful businessman with untold wealth in his future. Alice was comfortable with those disparities.

What she was looking for she found in his character. He was steady, vulnerable and gentle toward her in manner and speech. He wasn't brash, or boisterous or judgmental of others. Those appealing qualities would balance her occasional brashness and judgmentalism. In time, and with his high level of tolerance, Bob could mentor Alice how to convert those weaknesses into virtues. She welcomed this spiritual growth.

What she sought she found in him. It was everything she needed to rewrite the tragic story of her estrangement from her brother, Teddy. Even if that story were never rewritten, Alice had a sure instinct that Bob Cratchit's kind and amiable manner would assure her of never repeating such a chapter in her life. In Bob, she felt a way out of the inner prison of her years of remorse. That hope alone was worth the risk of entrusting that broken piece of her heart to Bob for healing.

Eventually, their weekends evolved into dinners, dancing, picnics in parks, Sunday services at St. Giles and strolling along the Thames. With each encounter, their hearts began to beat as one as they shared their dreams and hopes for the future.

One year after they began courting, Bob surprised Alice. "Who can I ask for your hand in marriage?"

"You can ask me, of course," Alice replied with both a smile and a devilish wink.

Bob was prepared with his own comeback line. "Thank you for making this easy."

In a courtly gesture, Bob genuflected on one knee, grabbed both of her hands softly and in a confident tone, asked, "Alice Clifton you will make me a happy man by becoming my wife."

Alice's reply startled Bob.

"Bob Cratchit, you will make me a happy woman by becoming my husband." Her grin inspired Bob to open his arms and embrace her in an endearing hug. Bob couldn't see the mischievous smile Alice wore. It was painted with thoughts of her rascal Aunt Joe who would have approved of her niece's clever acceptance of Bob's marriage proposal.

Their nuptials were held at St. Giles Church one year later on a beautiful Saturday in May, 1839. Bob had just turned twenty-five and Alice was twenty-six. Their one year age difference was not an issue. All that mattered was their unrequited love for each other and a strong mutual desire to honor their vows of growing that love into a family.

They picked the third weekend of May because it usually coincided with celebrating Queen Victoria's birthday. That meant Monday was a national holiday giving them a full two-day honeymoon.

Throughout their courtship, both of them withheld a private secret. For Bob it was a longing to father children who would rescue him from the years of having no siblings to love. For Alice it was releasing, for the sake of her future children, all the love held captive inside her but refused by her brother's failures to reconcile with her. She coveted the hope of soon ending her long nightmare by beginning a family with the release of such unused love.

During the year of their betrothal, Bob frugally budgeted money for their wedding and honeymoon. His parents helped with the expense of their reception. It was held under an ornate tent on the banks of the pond in Camden Town Park.

The fifty guests and the church vicar walked the short distance. A mild breeze and blossoming spring flowers helped to make the stroll a sacred pilgrimage. A wealthy client of Alice Cratchit, who owned an upscale restaurant, catered the nuptial luncheon. A string quartet added festive background music. Occasionally, they competed with the chorus of quacking geese who remained long enough to enjoy the spoils of uneaten food. Bob and Alice laughed the loudest as they invited their guests to throw a piece of wedding cake to the adoring, but noisy and uninvited wobbling and feathered guests.

They honeymooned in a charming cottage overlooking the white cliffs of Dover. They traveled the seventy-two miles on the evening train from Charing Cross Station and spent three days making love, making plans and making God happy with their strolls along the cliffs and sharing their private desires to embark on a long and happy life together.

The cottage was a modest two-story edifice, situated on two acres of land. The front of the house faced the sea. The breathtaking view of the English Channel overlooking the white cliffs of Dover was a most appealing characteristic worthy of bragging rights.

On Sunday they attended services at St. Mary of the Virgin Church. Then they strolled around the quaint seaside town. Both had heard pleasant stories about the special charm of Dover, but for them both this was their first visit to this region of Kent.

After dining at the cottage that evening they strolled along the cliffs inhaling the delight of the sea breeze until the sun set. Seated on a bench, in silence, they watched the sun fade into the west. As it gradually descended below the horizon it left enough energy to brighten each other's life with passionate love-making until they fell asleep in each other's arms.

On Monday, they toured the famous Dover Castle perched on the hill over-looking the city. They learned that it originally was called by the French name of the River Dour that flows through the village. But, the English translation of Dover has been used since Shakespeare wrote *King Lear* between 1604 and 1606. The town and its famous chalk cliffs play a prominent role in the tragic play. Shakespeare Cliff, high above the enclosed port, was named after the bard in appreciation for the recognition he gave the town in his literary tragedy.

"I studied *King Lear* in secondary school. It's not an upbeat play," Alice commented as they strolled through the castle arm in arm. "I don't know how much good it does the town, to name a cliff after a great literary author whose writings were mostly about human suffering and tragedy."

Bob was petulant in his reply. "Well, my dear, we can only hope that the town's kindness and hospitality toward us is expressive of how they're attempting to rewrite the story to fit the local charms."

This was Bob's way of recognizing how people-friendly the citizens have been during their honeymoon.

"I am so smitten by the historical sights and pleasant faces of Dover that I look forward to our visiting here again." He paused before adding:

"Perhaps we should celebrate every wedding anniversary here to replay the memories of our honeymoon and the role that Dover is playing in our love story."

When Alice heard these words she tightened her grip around Bob's arm. He immediately absorbed the warmth of her approval.

Try as they did to keep Shakespeare's proclivity for dark and sad playwriting out of their lives, eventually tragedy would enter their married bliss and bring them back to Dover for healing and renewed hope.

$\mathcal{S}$ix years after Alice gave birth to Tim, she was surprised to learn that she was once again pregnant. The rhythm of being tutor and cheerleader to Tim, as well as loving mother to three growing children, was about to be interrupted. This news was something neither she nor Bob expected. Grappling with all the issues of surrounding this surprise, they both kept themselves open to the deeper mystery of what God was unfolding in their lives. Bob was concerned with the economic issues of an addition to the family, while Alice was worried about her advancing age. At thirty-six, her health and energy had been tested by years of special care for Tim. Puzzling and straining questions consumed her. Could her diminished stamina withstand the physical ordeal of pregnancy? Could she be as devoted a mother to a new child at thirty-six as she was to her first child at twenty-seven?

As the months passed, every member of the Cratchit family adjusted to Alice's changing moods and worries. Shortly before her delivery, Alice quietly harbored suspicions about the unborn child that paralleled those that preceded the birth of Tiny Tim. Her female instincts told her something was wrong.

During ten hours of labor her contractions grew more painful. The child was not assisting in its own birth. Alice wailed and prayed aloud, desperate for a miracle. Bob could only hope for the best as he suffered through the ordeal, hearing her cries from a cold waiting room. At a point of near physical exhaustion Alice delivered a stillborn child. She wept interminably. Bob held her in his arms, comforting her with his own tears.

The newly-converted Ebenezer Scrooge paid for the infant's burial and offered Bob an extended leave to comfort his grieving wife.

The grieving couple returned to their Dover honeymoon cottage for rest and recovery. The pastoral atmosphere, with daily walks along the white cliffs and the breeze of the salt air, were healing balms for the unexpected loss of a daughter they named Estella.

The tragedy of King Lear's loss of a favorite daughter had cast a shadow over their idyllic lives. It left Alice haunted by Shakespeare's searing prediction: *"When we are born, we cry that we are come to this great stage of fools."*

CHAPTER 6

Peter Cratchit

*Y*oung Peter Crachit was every bit his father's son. They had the same gentle disposition, soft-spoken voice, and kind-hearted nature. These virtues fueled a unique kind of compassion that enabled Peter to interact easily with children of the parents in the Marshalsea. One particular child, the son of a chronic debtor, pushed Peter's care and compassion to the limits. His name was Clive McPherson. At first he shunned all attempts to become friends out of pure jealousy for Peter's blessings.

Peter capitalized on his virtues by never shunning Clive. While Bob visited with Mr. McPherson, Peter attempted to engage his angry son.

"Clive, would you like to play some soccer in the courtyard?"

"I'm not an athlete and I don't like being laughed at."

"I'm not athletic either so I won't laugh at you if you won't laugh at me." Peter waited for Clive to answer but all he got was a stare. He decided to become a storyteller.

"On Sundays our family invites a guest to dinner. Would you be my guest some Sunday?"

"Is this your way of taking pity on me?"

"No Clive, it's my way of being friendly. Just like our dads have done, I like making new friends." Peter followed Clive's lead in a gentle manner.

Clive's silence gave Peter hope. Eventually, Clive spoke.

"Being in prison has softened my dad. I can see him changing. I'm still angry for all the years he was never friendly towards me."

Peter was surprised by Clive's attempt at vulnerability. He chose his words carefully.

"I would like to help change that Clive by developing a friendship with you."

Clive lowered his head, not in shame, but in a pondering manner.

"I guess Sunday dinner is a good place to start."

Peter's smile said everything. As they walked closer to the prison court-yard, he began bouncing the soccer ball until they started kicking it.

During these adolescent years, the experiences during the prison visits mirrored for Peter and Clive what Bob's steady and kind nature did to change Ebenezer Scrooge.

The two young boys became the best of friends. In time, Clive's animosity toward his father softened. It was the beginning of a new chapter in their relationship as father and son.

The first time Scrooge met Clive was at a Sunday dinner at the Cratchits. The converted miser and the converted bully become friends. As Scrooge listened to Clive's story, he envisioned a social issue that touched his heart. Eventually, the two became advocates for reform for welfare standards of displaced children who were orphaned, or whose parents were imprisoned.

Their efforts helped change the workhouse model of child care. It was replaced with residential institutions.

With generous funds from some initial philanthropists, the first orphanages were built. Peter's example with Clive inspired Ebenezer Scrooge to leave a bequest in his will as seed money for an orphanage. These were nothing like the Victorian workhouses showcased in Dickens', *"Oliver Twist."* No characters like Fagin (a conniving career criminal), Bill Sikes (a brutal burglar) or the Artful Dodger (a clever pickpocket) ever occupied those orphanages. They only existed in Dickens's imagination.

In the last years prior to college, Peter gained Clive's trust as a tutor. His story is as different from Peter's story as Venus is different from Mars. But Peter welcomed the challenge Clive's Belfast bravado presented. Both were seventeen, but their similarities ended there.

Whereas Peter's personality was calming and polished, Clive's was harsh and rough-edged. Peter was raised to be a gentleman. Clive was raised to be hostile. Peter's family was genuinely cohesive. Clive's family was brutally dysfunctional. Peter was prone to be a peacemaker. Clive was raised to be a bully.

It was precisely these personality disparities that mysteriously drew Peter to Clive. Peters' stable and indulgent nature enabled him to see the good in Clive that Clive couldn't see in himself due to his ugly and shadowy past. It took every ounce of compassion in Peter to withstand the nasty lines that Clive spat at him for nearly a year. Clive's foulness masked years of anger toward his father's laziness and bad choices. As Clive eventually ran out of energy trying to be a bully, Peter melted his brutal behavior with endless reserves of patience and a steadiness, all the while maintaining his dignity.

Those virtues were the weapons that wore Clive down and awakened in him a new desire to acquire them for himself. This turning point for Peter was tantamount to watching his adopted Uncle Scrooge change from an abrasive miser into a caring man. Peter felt a growing need to share Clive's conversion with his father.

After returning from their Marshalsea visit one Saturday, the maturing seventeen-year old Peter huddled with his father around the fireplace. Sharing a quiet moment, Peter broke their reverenced silence with an ear-catching comment.

"Papa, today Clive asked a question that gave me some hope that he longs for a change of attitude."

"What was his question, Peter?"

"He asked how I am able to be so calm when he treats me with such resentment."

Bob leaned into the fire to light a wax taper.

"How did you answer him, son," Bob asked as he lit the candles on the mantelpiece to brighten the parlor.

"I answered him by asking what he thought it meant that he was asking me that particular question."

Bob took a moment to ponder Peter's question.

"He said that being angry all the time was tiring him out and that my being calm was showing him another way to live by using that energy to get along with people."

Bob beamed with delight. "I'm very proud of you Peter. Something tells me this is not the end of Clive's story."

"I think you're right, Papa," Peter replied, "and I hope it ends better than the way it started."

Peter Cratchit was fourteen years old when Ebenezer Scrooge had his Christmas Eve life changing experience. From then on Mr. Scrooge was no longer a strange anomaly to the Cratchit family. Rather, he became the adopted uncle the children did not have. For the final two years of Peter's secondary schooling, Scrooge showed keen interest in his facility for math. He coached Peter in the art of accounting, thus sowing in him seeds of interest in making finance and business a life career.

Bob and Alice Cratchit gave Scrooge their blessing in his role as mentor to Peter. It would earn dividends for everyone, especially Scrooge who was quietly and unexpectedly learning new ethical business standards from Peter while in his capacity as tutor.

As Peter's commencement from secondary school neared, Scrooge cleverly approached the subject of college during dinner one evening with Peter and his parents.

"Peter, what are your plans after school for continuing to develop into a gentleman?"

Peter engaged Scrooge's question with budding confidence.

"Thanks to you, Uncle Scrooge, I wish to pursue a career in some field of finance and accounting, but I am not sure what specialty that will be."

Peter's response opened the door for Scrooge to propose a plan that he had been developing, and that he hoped would be well received by everyone.

"Peter, I would like to propose that you study at the University College of London to get the clarity you need about what area of business best suits you for a career. If you accept this proposal, with your parent's permission, then I would award you the first Scrooge & Marley scholarship. It will be enough to pay for your college education."

While Bob and Alice sat in stunned silence at the table, Peter was animated.

"Uncle Scrooge, I happily accept your proposal and scholarship. I will make you proud of me." He looked to his parents who signaled approval.

As they all stood and toasted the good news with glasses of port, Peter added, "If it is meant to be, then I hope someday, Uncle Scrooge, to utilize my college education with your firm. I have some ideas about how to expand the business by establishing foundations for some charitable causes."

As Scrooge's smile widened, he respectfully bowed his head. "Let's all drink to that."

CHAPTER 7

*I*n the fall of 1858, Peter Cratchit registered as a freshman at the University College of London. Thanks to caring parents and the tutelage of Ebenezer Scrooge, Peter was well prepared for the academic transition to college life. Serious in his study habits, he equally displayed a quality of independent thinking when engaging professors in the classroom. He had a high level of enthusiasm about the rapid pace of the industrial revolution and his unconventional ideas for new business ventures earned him favorable impressions. Naturally, a few professors voiced skepticism about his free-style thinking habits, preferring that he conform to the textbook theories and practices. However, even those doubters were charmed by Peter's skillful art of business diplomacy. Far from being Machaivellian, he endeared himself by his sincere and genuine style of honest engagement.

His first year of studies focused on the fundamentals of accounting, ethical standards in business practices and the ever evolving subject of drafting contractual agreements.

In his second year of college Peter met a student, literally by running into him. They were in different stacks of the library and, both being distracted, collided into each other as they exited in opposite directions.

In an apologetic, but comedic tone, the student reached out his hand and said, "I'm Abner Solomon and believe it or not this isn't my usual way of introduction."

Peter laughed and said, "I'm Peter Cratchit and I like your style."

As they collected the books and papers that had scattered at the point of their collision, Peter invited his new friend to join him for a pint at Wickfield's Pub, the local watering hole.

As they chatted over pints of different ales, they discovered they were both pursuing a Baccalaureate degree in business.

Peter, being a self-initiator, spoke freely and positively about his loving family.

"I wouldn't be here having this conversation if it weren't for my parents. They were very zealous in our education. I am the beneficiary of all my father has learned from his boss, Mr. Ebenezer Scrooge. Since his mid-life change years ago, Mr. Scrooge, became my adopted uncle. Thanks to a scholarship he established I am able to attend college and chart a career in business."

Peter spoke passionately about the mentoring he received from his 'Uncle Scrooge.' Abner listened quietly hiding his resentment.

"It has made my transition to college all the more smooth and exciting."

While Peter rambled, Abner Solomon absorbed his story with more than just sharp ears. His mind was storing the information with the aptitude of a bookkeeper entering figures, flawlessly, into a ledger. His ear fine-tuned when he heard the name Ebenezer Scrooge.

When Peter peppered him with questions about his family and educational history, Abner skillfully deflected attention by asking questions to elicit more information from Peter instead. He exhibited a particular interest in Martha.

"If your sister is anything like you, she must be doubly interesting," Abner commented in a veiled sinister expression.

Peter didn't catch the implication and sallied on about Martha's virtues.

"We're more different that we are alike. She doesn't see herself in the domestic sphere. She was recently hired as a clerk at a milliner store on Oxford Street with the goal to be the manager in four years. With her outgoing personality and business sense, I give her two years." Peter chuckled as if he were pretending to read Martha's palm.

"She has a plan to open her own brand of milliner shops and is determined to be successful," Peter spoke with obvious pride in his sister.

"What about marriage? Is that in her plan someday," Abner asked feigning innocence.

Peter's answer was not exactly what Abner was anticipating. "My sister will not cultivate a relationship that may end in an unhappy marriage."

"If marriage is in her plan then it will be at her time and on her terms. She is not the submissive type, so such a man would have to be flexible and adapt to her priorities and her understanding of marital roles."

Peter paused before adding, "My parents raised her to be very independent and that is not an issue of compromise for her."

Abner's eyes tightened as he limited his response to a nod of his head. His next line evoked a smile from Peter.

"I look forward to meeting her someday. She sounds like the kind of person an adventurous guy like me would enjoy. Also, I prefer challenging woman to boring ones."

. After they went their separate ways, Peter pondered the unsettling feeling that Abner left knowing far more about him than Peter knew about Abner. He brushed it off as the initial frets and fears about the mystery of growing new friendships.

They met again on Saturday for Vespers at the university chapel followed by more pints and dinner at Wickfield's Pub. This time the ale worked its magic on Abner, rendering him much more animated about his family life and his goals.

"My father is the founder of Solomon & Company. It's a small loan and investment company. While not on the same scale of prominence as Scrooge & Marley, he is building a reputation for investing in the waves of industrial growth. My one and only older brother bypassed college and went to work for my father after secondary school. I chose college as I have more ambitious plans."

Peter gleaned more personal information out of Abner as he gradually teetered toward intoxication. He saw no glow in his new friend as he talked about his family. Rather, Abner contrived a portrait of a family who was disciplined, distant, stiff and formal. While Peter addressed his father affectionately as "Papa," Abner spoke of his "Father." The omission of family traditions celebrating holidays, birthdays, and Christmas pulled at Peter's heartstrings leading him to envision a family without celebratory or spiritual glue to bind them together.

Little did Abner know that sharing details of his family history of rigidity and orthodoxy while becoming intoxicated did not impress Peter. It left him questioning Abner's aspirations as far as developing a relationship with the happy, infectious and self-reliant Martha Cratchit?

Peter left feeling sympathetic about the absence of warmth in Abner's family ties. He balanced it with a sense of wonder about whether Abner was disguising a desperate plea for this new friendship to help Abner change his life story. The question haunted Peter as he assisted Abner back to his rented quarters. After several stumbles and falls, he finally got him to bed and left him, fully clothed, alone to nurse his drunken stupor.

The next day Abner was noticeably absent from class.

CHAPTER 8

Martha Cratchit

*M*artha Cratchit grew up in a house where she was outnumbered three to one. She eschewed playing with dolls, dressing up and pretending to host high tea parties. While she developed her own mystique as a woman, she wove into her gender a fierce independent streak that put men on notice that she was no one's slave. She inherited this quality of inner freedom from her free-thinking mother. Her father augmented it with pride for her ambitiousness and unique sense of self-worth.

Both parents instilled in Martha a sense of compassion for the poor and destitute. Her longing heart for justice, when combined with the folly and foibles of the world as it spun towards a new decade, nurtured a unique authenticity in her. When she turned nineteen she exuded a dignity that whenever she appeared in public it was equated to an "announcement"…" Martha Cratchit has arrived."

The one feminine thing that captured her imagination early in life was hats. Hats, for Martha, were more than just fashion accessories. They were an exclamation point at the end of a declarative statement that spoke volumes about their wearer's character and destined to raise curiosity as well as eyebrows.

As Martha shared her dream of one day owning a store, Bob Cratchit was gentle in breaking the news that women in Victorian England were denied the rights of ownership, when it came to business.

"Dream slowly, Martha! Hopefully, those laws will change in pace with your hopes and dreams.

"Someday, Papa, they will change and you can count on me to help bring it about."

Bob refrained from criticism believing that her statement was more prophetic than stereotypical of women whose rights were legally tethered to a husband. The idea that she was legal tender to any man was abhorrent to Martha.

When it came to marriage, Martha's plan was to become a business woman first and a wife, second. If she couldn't find the right man who shared her views of marriage as a partnership, she would settle for being a single woman married to and finding happiness in her business.

After completing secondary school, and working at a milliner store for three years, she shared her plan with Uncle Ebenezer.

They met at his office. She was keenly aware that he would respect her choice of environment to discuss her business matters. She arrived early and he was impressed with her punctuality.

"What brings my favorite adopted niece to my office today," Scrooge asked in a teasing voice.

"While I appreciate your flattery, uncle, the truth is I am your *only* niece."

Scrooge increased his flattery skills with a wide smile. "And that makes your visit all the more pleasant, my dear." Then clearing his throat, he assumed a more formal tone.

"You mentioned a business proposal. I am anxious to hear it."

She dug deep into her inner well of confidence and presented her proposition like a veteran entrepreneur, young in age but wise in vision.

"I have a plan to open a milliner shop. I know of a vacant building on Bond Street, an ideal location for shoppers. I intend to woo women with a variety of hats and other apparels, including some of my own designs."

The art of not losing eye contact with Scrooge increased his respect for her poise and her plan. Also, her economy of words made good impressions.

"I need a loan from you to buy that building and the capital to start the business, but more than that I need you to be a benefactor who will sign for the deed and believe in my dream and help bring it to life with your moral support."

She paused. Scrooge gave her the space to form her thoughts into words.

"I am asking you to be a business partner until such time as I can stand on my own."

Martha anticipated Scrooge's first question and was prepared with a ready answer.

"Have you discussed this matter with your parents?"

"Yes, uncle, and they are supportive of my dream of being a business woman and of my meeting with you today."

"Then I shall be supportive too," Scrooge replied to the delight of Martha's ears. His added thoughts grew an ever-widening smile on her face.

"Sooner or later this unjust impediment of denying woman the right to ownership of a business must change. By partnering with you Martha, my colleagues will know on what side of the issue I stand, and hopefully, will join in the efforts to hasten that change."

"I will have a clerk in the loan department draft an agreement. I will set the loan of one thousand pounds repayable in five years. If you repay it sooner, that will be considered as interest which can be applied toward opening a second store. Are those terms agreeable, Martha?"

"Yes uncle and I will add a promise not to let you down."

Scrooge had the last word. "I will hold you to that though I trust your word. Let us toast our business arrangement with a glass of brandy."

Following their meeting, Scrooge treated his young, enchanting business partner to lunch in the dining room of Mansfield House. He hand-picked the elegant hotel on the edge of Kensington Gardens to celebrate their new capital venture. Over libations and kidney pie, they solidified their partnership. It left Martha feeling contented in the assurance of a new career, and it left Scrooge feeling all the younger by a maturing woman whose charm and confidence melted any resistance he may have had to her business plan. After all, he thought while walking back to his office, "everything begins with a dream."

CHAPTER 9

Peter Cratchit

ix months before the completion of college, Peter made an appointment with the Academic Dean to make sure his records were in order for graduation in the spring of 1862. Over the past three years, he had worked during breaks at Scrooge & Marley. It gave him a distinct advantage by rooting his feet firmly in the world of finance and business.

The Dean's secretary caught his eye. She had a countenance that seemed untouched by time and radiated both elegance and resoluteness while engaging Peter in conversation.

"Dean Spencer is in a meeting and has asked that you please wait. He will be available shortly." The tenderness of her voice made her beauty seem immutable. While Peter breathed in all her exquisite features, he smiled inside knowing that Martha would approve of the young lady's unique apparel. It was clear that she was not an archetypal Victorian woman.

Uncomfortable simply waiting in silence, Peter leaned on his self-confidence.

"My name is Peter Cratchit." Her response was unanticipated.

"Yes, I know, you are Dean Spencer's one o'clock appointment."

"I'm sorry, but I don't know your name."

Eying him directly, she replied, "I am Abigail Langley." Then, to his dismay she added, "Is there anything else you would like to know." They chatted amiably until the Dean opened his office door and invited Peter in.

Six months later, Abigail had a reserved seat with the Cratchit family for Peter's commencement. Privy to his academic records, she already knew that he had been chosen to deliver the Salutatory address to the class and she admired his humility in not boasting about the honor. It was a piece of his character that charmed her off her feet.

Peter and Abigail courted for over a year. Their families became close as their affections for one another deepened. The two had much in common, but also valued each other's differences that made them special. While Peter became established as a junior clerk at the firm of Scrooge and Marley, Abigail continued making first-rate impressions in the executive offices of the university. Following a betrothal ceremony at St. Giles Church, they were married in the spring of 1864 in the Church of St. Martin-in-the-Fields. They honeymooned in the same cottage where Bob and Alice had consummated their marital love years earlier. A third Cratchit now had some affinity with the romantic cottage overlooking the white cliffs of Dover.

Abner Solomon was a guest at the wedding, as was Clive McPherson, who served as an usher. While Peter was distracted with his new bride, Abner took the liberty of surprising Martha with an invitation to dance. Martha obliged, and four dances later she was exhausted. Refilling their champagne glasses, Abner invited her to stroll in the gardens of the reception venue. Martha agreed to join Abner for a string quartet concert at the Royal Conservatory the following weekend.

Peter, who had noticed his sister's absence, interrupted the budding romance with an unusually brusque comment. "We are getting ready to cut the wedding cake, so please come along before someone gets your pieces."

Peter feigned interest all the while feeling unsettled about Abner's motives. He had concluded that the glue to cement a relationship between Abner and his sister was lacking, since both their character and their dreams were quite different.

Peter quietly promised to himself to be protective of Martha from whatever aspirations or claims Abner had in mind for his only sister. After several months, as Martha and Abner's relationship blossomed, Peter broached the subject with her.

"How serious is your relationship with Abner?"

"Are you asking as a caring brother or do you harbor some other motive?" Martha displayed her mother's penchant for making a point quickly.

"As your brother I care about your happiness."

"What makes you think I may be unhappy about this budding relationship?"

"My instincts tell me that you are two different people with different goals."

"On what do you base that critique?"

"You have grown into an unconventional woman. I am proud of you for that Martha. But I have a sense that Abner is looking for a woman more suited to his traditional values."

"What makes you say that, Peter?"

"He shared with me some personal details about his family. They do not have the warmth, freedom and intimacy that we have. You may not know that because I would guess that you have not yet been introduced to his family."

Peter paused to choose his words delicately. Martha obliged.

"I fear he may have expectations of you that you will not be able to meet, especially on the subject of a woman being submissive to a man. I know how uncompromising you are on that issue. Please be cautious Martha. I don't want you to get hurt."

Martha reached over, and gently kissed her older brother on the cheek. "You have conveyed your warning as care. Thank you for that."

Peter returned her affection with a kiss on her cheek. He knew his words would rest in her heart and would be quickly accessed when and if the time was appropriate.

CHAPTER 10

Scrooge & Peter

*O*n the fifth anniversary of his full employment at Scrooge & Cratchit, Peter was summoned into his uncle's office. It was unanticipated, so naturally, Peter felt a bit displaced.

"I want to wish you 'Happy Anniversary' at the firm." "Since I now enjoy rewarding employees for their loyal service, I thought the best gift I could give for this occasion is a promotion."

Peter's eyes widened, blinking utter surprise at what he had just heard.

"Effective the next pay day, you are hereby a senior clerk in the firm of Scrooge & Cratchit. Are you up to this task?"

"Yes sir, I am and I will continue to make you proud of my loyalty to the company."

"That's what I want to hear," Scrooge replied. "I'm offering you this promotion because of your sharp vision for enticing new investors in the modernization of England triggered by this second industrial revolution."

Scrooge proceeded to itemize the breadth of Peter's business acumen with the added capital it had brought to the company.

"You have persuaded new clients to invest their wealth in areas of modernization that I would not have envisioned. Our firm is now at the forefront of underwriting great changes in the textile industry. Thanks to your efforts the Wyatt Textile Mills in Birmingham are flourishing."

Scrooge continued listing Peter's accomplishments as if he were reciting a litany of praise.

"Thanks to you our ventures in the production of cast iron in the Liverpool factories are modernizing our infrastructure with iron bridges. Thanks to you investors have quadrupled in venturing in steam-powered railways. Thanks to you, the labyrinth of canals being planned and dug has improved the pace of transporting materials to the industrial centers. You anticipated before any other investment firm, the mass production of machinery making it faster for the workforce to keep pace with economic growth."

Scrooge saved his best accolade for last.

"Your vision, perseverance and dedication have placed Scrooge and Cratchit at the forefront of increasing the standard of living for the general population. We are held in high esteem by our colleagues in the stock exchange because of your unconventional imagination in the business world. I foresee that you will be a pioneer in the emergence of a new modern economy in the next century."

Scrooge became sentimental in his closing remarks.

"I won't live to see that day, but I am content that my mentoring and influence of your worldview will help to make that change happen."

As Scrooge stood from his chair, a grateful Peter did the same. Deferring from a traditional handshake, he embraced Peter with a hug that was reserved for a father and son.

He whispered into Peter's ear, "You have earned my pride and this promotion honorably, and I couldn't be happier if you were my own son."

Scrooge invited Bob into his office. After sharing the news, the three men beamed with pride while toasting a glass of brandy.

CHAPTER 11

Peter & Abigail

One year into their marriage, Abigail was with child. Bob and Alice couldn't be happier at the anticipation of becoming grandparents. Peter was delighted with the thought of parenting after the model of his father. Martha and Tim were intoxicated with the thought of becoming an aunt and uncle. Ebenezer Scrooge was cheerful about the thought of another young Cratchit adding sparkle to his aging, but contented life.

When it was time for Abigail to leave her post at the University, Peter became very attentive to his wife's physical needs. Their first child was born on Queen Victoria's birthday, prompting them to name him Victor to honor the occasion. He was the pride of every Cratchit and Langley, awaiting their first grandchild. He was also the joy of an adopted great uncle whose quality of life was enriched with new cheer in the declining years of his life. Scrooged relished the sound of a crying baby echoing through the empty rooms of his house whenever they visited.

By the time Victor was born in 1865, Scrooge had dissolved the firm of Scrooge and Marley and legally reconstituted it as the firm of Scrooge and Cratchit. In addition to earning the title of senior partner, Bob Cratchit's salary and dividends had quadrupled. The increased earnings, coupled with a sizeable yearly bonus enabled him to purchase the Dover cottage that he and Alice held in such a cherished place in their hearts. Alice turned younger redecorating it. In her mind it would be the dream home-by-the-sea where she and Bob would live their retirement years. Also, it would be the getaway house from an ever sprawling and noisy London city where the family could gather for holidays.

Two years after Scrooge promoted Bob to senior partner, he surprised Peter with his second promotion.

Once again, the converted mild-mannered founder of the firm left Peter speechless a second time.

"I'm recalling a dividend on my investment in your education by promoting you to the position of junior partner. Are you up to this task?"

"If you recall how I honored your first promotion, uncle, then please know that I am confident of making you doubly proud of this second promotion."

Peter celebrated his promotion by taking his wife to dinner. He shared his good news in a playful manner.

"Abigail, what do you think about having another child? Victor is two years old and for all we know he is waiting for a brother or a sister."

"Can we afford a second child right now, Peter?"

"I was promoted today to junior partner, so I confidently say, 'Yes' we can very well afford another child." Sounding mischievous he added, "...or two, or three."

Abigail giggled as her eyes ballooned with surprise. "Oh Peter, I am so proud of you. Pay the check quickly," she giggled, "so we can get home and turn our joy into lovemaking for a new child."

Peter's comeback line painted a pleasantly wicked face on his adoring wife.

"I have a better idea, sweetheart. Let's spend the weekend making love at the cottage in Dover. Who knows it might be wild enough to give birth to a set of twins!"

They laughed heartily and toasted their new dream with a glass of tasty French champagne.

CHAPTER 12

Bob & Alice Cratchit

Five years after Bob's promotion as senior partner, and with Scrooge in declining health, Bob and Alice began spending more cherished time at their Dover cottage. Bob presided at an informal ritual to celebrate the placement of a sign naming the cottage *Clift Side*. The name contained the double entendre - of his spouse's maiden name, *Clifton*, as well as the position of the cottage at the edge of one of the famed white cliffs of Dover. Underneath the name was the word "Welcome" painted by Bob and Alice's loving hands.

Alice busied herself with interior decorations that endowed the cottage with a more Cratchit-friendly environment. In the first five years they enlarged the dining area to accommodate their growing family. A horseshoe addition at the rear of the cottage included a nursery and two guest suites so their grandchildren could entertain them during visits. They installed the modern convenience of indoor plumbing. A master suite and a guest room were neatly laid out on the second floor. A Jacobean staircase was cleverly installed to assure maximum use of the narrow hallway for welcoming guests inside the front door.

A gallery of framed pictures on shelves, walls and mantelpieces containing faces and memories of weddings, baptisms and family gatherings at the cottage provided finishing touches to several different rooms. The planting of a flower garden – the one unfinished item on Alice's check list - inspired her to muse, "hopefully, very soon."

The more time the doting couple spent in Dover, the more involved they became in the community. Bob was elected to the Vestry of St. Mary of the Virgin Church and Alice was appointed to the governing board of the local hospital, which was opened just five years earlier. Inspired by her son's health struggles, Alice steered the board's growth and vision into the creation of a pediatric ward for children with physical disabilities and communicable diseases. Shortly after the dedication, Alice was honored with a plaque at the entrance to the ward.

Alice did more than just attend board meetings. She visited patients regularly, particularly those with whom she had something in common: estrangement from their family or no one to bring them companionship, comfort or flowers.

One cold winter day at the hospital she stumbled upon a middle-aged couple. The woman was lying in a bed overcome with sadness, her eyes reddened by heavy weeping. A man sat next to her holding her hand while softly chanting prayers.

Not wanting to intrude on their space, she sat quietly, her presence intended to offer comfort without words. Eventually, he introduced himself.

The man bowed respectfully. "My name is Oliver McCready." While shifting his glance toward the patient, he continued. "This is my wife, Magdalena." Alice immediately detected an Irish accent.

"I am Alice Cratchit," she said softly. "Can I do anything to make your stay more comfortable?"

"Thank you for asking," Oliver said. To her astonishment, he shared a story that opened the floodgates of Alice's heart.

"We are both from Ireland, born out of wedlock and raised in different orphanages. We were so ill-treated by Catholic nuns and brothers that when we were of age to leave, the only thing we left behind was our faith."

Alice could almost tangibly feel the emotional scars the religious men and women inflicted on them.

Never letting go of his wife's hand, Oliver continued his storytelling in a reverent voice.

"Eventually, we immigrated to England and were hired by a wealthy British Lord to work on his country estate near Grassemere in the Lake District. I became the head gardener and Magdalena became housekeeper. We married after getting settled there."

Oliver deeply inhaled a new supply of energy to continue.

"We both longed for children, though Magdalena was worried about bearing children at age thirty-five. Eventually, God blessed us with twin girls. Healed of our orphanage scars, we reconciled with the Catholic Church and had the girls baptized. Eight months later, during a visit to London, they were abducted outside Kings Cross Station while we were distracted with a couple who, we later learned, were decoys in the kidnapping ruse."

Focusing on his wife, Oliver tightened his grip on her hand. She blinked approval with an almost angelic face.

"We remained in London for a month hoping that Scotland Yard would find our beloved girls. With our money running out we returned to the north, but our lives were so broken and empty without the girls that we couldn't remain there."

"We have been in Dover for a month. Our plan was to catch a ferry to France to get as far away from our loss and sadness as possible. Shortly after we arrived, Magdalena collapsed from exhaustion and a broken heart. I have spent all our savings on her hospital care and now share a room at the Mercy House for travelers a short distance from the ferry port. I have no choice but to live one day at a time and rely on the mercy of God."

Alice steeled herself from the urge to weep a river of tears. She engaged Oliver with the purpose of restoring his empty life with new hope.

"Mr. McCready, I am both touched and saddened by your story. Thank you for sharing it with me. The mercy of God sent me here to visit you today. I will return tomorrow with some news that may give you hope. I bid the Lord to keep you both in his care until then."

Before exiting, Alice bowed respectfully to Oliver and bent low to place a gentle kiss on Magdalena's forehead. Her almost trance-like state seemed to melt as she beamed a warm smile.

That evening during dinner, Alice shared with Bob the story of this most meaningful encounter. "With careful planning," she conceded, "we could hire Oliver as a gardener and caretaker, and Magdalena as housekeeper."

Bob pondered her words while slowly enjoying the delicious pot roast Alice had prepared for dinner. She interpreted his silence as permission to continue.

"It would not be inconvenient for them to occupy one of the guest rooms by the nursery. What do you think, my dear Robert?" Bob raised his wine glass. "I think you just found a solution to your dream of having a garden. Shall we toast to that?" Alice was charmed by her husband's humor and compassion.

The next day Bob joined Alice at the hospital to share the news about their wishes to hire the couple to work at *Clift Side Cottage.*

As Bob spoke, Oliver could not contain his tears. Magdalena used her blanket to wipe them from his eyes. To everyone's surprise she spoke.

"Mr. and Mrs. Cratchit, my husband's tears are telling me this is a miracle and that we should not turn our backs on it. We gladly accept your offer and look forward to our continued healing in your employ. Please send us information about the cottage and we will visit by week's end."

Anticipating some released joy for the occasion Alice brought a vase of fresh flowers and placed them on the table next to Magdalena's bed. They worked their magic quickly as a colorful hue framed her countenance and a warm smile added a noticeable glow to her face.

As they returned to the cottage in their carriage, Alice snuggled close to Bob. She buried her hands deeper into her muff while leaning her head affectionately on her husband's shoulder. The intimacy of the moment warmed them from the cold air whispering around them. They both glowed inside with the blessed assurance that God was pleased with their works of mercy today. Why else, Alice contemplated would the Creator reward them with a full moon and sparkling stars dancing above their cottage that night?

CHAPTER 13

Tim Cratchit

*U*nlike his two effervescent siblings, Tim Cratchit endured a plethora of physical disabilities and ailments. He transitioned to adulthood only with the benefit of years of courage received from a concerned family and a rare supply of fortitude. He morphed into a gentleman with a special brand of patience and understanding toward children whose stories of suffering and pain were similar to his own. It came as no surprise that he chose medicine as a career. For half his life he had been pinched, prodded, needled and examined by enough doctors and nurses to staff a small hospital. Tim expressed it best himself:

"Our home and all the doctor and clinic visits were the laboratories where I developed my calling, as well as the bed side manners, for practicing my healing skills."

Tim's sad childhood story had taken a decidedly fortunate turn following Ebenezer Scrooge's mysterious Christmas Eve transformation of 1850. Tim had just turned eleven years old. Scrooge's inner awakening helped him to see Tim with a re-calibrated heart.

As the miser-turned-convert got comfortable with a transformed heart beating with compassion, he volunteered his financial help to Bob for the care of Tiny Tim. Somehow Scrooge knew his extreme spiritual make-over offered him a final chance to rescript his life. He never revealed to anyone how the spirit of Christmas-yet-to-come showed him an empty grave and epitaph that awakened his imagination to live a more purposeful life.

Tim Cratchit became the focus for Scrooge to unearth that new purpose and to live it with abandon. The more time he spent with the Cratchit's, the more he breathed in their love for each other and their kindness to strangers. He was especially touched by Tim's inner radiance during the season of Christmas. Uncle Ebenezer took great delight in telling others that Tiny Tim's line, "God bless us, everyone" was instrumental for permanently burying, "Bah, Humbug!"

When Tim was fourteen, Bob and Alice brought him to Belgium where he was examined in a clinic for people with spinal injuries and was placed in plaster of Paris traction, a technique that had been discovered just six years prior. Tim remained immobile for two months in the stifling summer European heat, but bore his discomfort without complaint. After it was removed, and they returned to London, Tim garnered Scrooge's attention daily sharing stories of "his Belgium Adventure."

"Uncle Ebenezer, Brussels is so different from London. Every day the nurses wheeled me onto a balcony to enjoy the view of the city. I left walking better and I hope to return again to see all that I missed."

Scrooge beamed with pride every time Tim addressed him as "Uncle." He listened intently, allowing the mystical light within Tiny Tim to warm his new desires for humble care giving. Scrooge never voiced the slightest hint for seeking recognition as the underwriter for their trip and Tim's hospital bill. He was paid in other manifold ways, such as Tim's gifts for awakening in Scrooge new longings for a middle aged man to be child-like again by mimicking Tim's simple and kind-hearted nature. Scrooge felt younger every day as he noticed how the desires to share Tim's innate optimism bore fruit in his own life.

"I am charmed by your stories of Brussels, Tim. You make me want to visit there someday." Scrooge found Tim's stories infectious.

When Tim completed secondary education in 1861, he was awarded the Scrooge & Marley scholarship to University College London. He studied a pre-med program, concentrating in human sciences, chemistry, biology, anatomy, and ethics. When he graduated in 1865, Scrooge sat with the family at the hooding ceremony. It gave legitimacy to his title as "Uncle."

Two years prior to his commencement, Queen Victoria signed a charter giving the university the right to grant degrees in surgery. Tim was accepted into the three-year program and was formally awarded a Doctor of Medical Science degree in 1868.

Two years prior to passing the required examinations to perform surgery, Tim met a surgical nurse-in-training. Julianne Manette was as intensely focused on her nursing studies as Tim was in his training to be a surgeon. Her father, Dr. Nathan Manette, chief of surgical medicine at the university, developed a fondness for Tim, finding him to be a serious student, disciplined, persevering and blest with authentically kind and warm bedside manners. His regard for Tim soared when the young doctor-in-training shared with the esteemed teacher his health history, the years of treatment he endured and the care and nurturing he received from his parents and siblings. Dr. Manette often expressed an eagerness to meet Tim's family.

"You are blest to have had such a loving family. I am sure their attention and affection to your needs hastened your healing. I hope I have the privilege of meeting them."

"We keep a tradition of gathering for Sunday dinner as often as possible," Tim said proudly. "We would be honored to have you at our dinner table."

Dr. Manette's likeness morphed into favoritism when Tim expressed interest in dating his daughter.

"Dr. Manette, I would like to ask if you have any objections to my courting your daughter."

Not only did the good doctor give Tim his blessing, but he polished his mischievous skills as a matchmaker. With surgical precision, Dr. Manette orchestrated the courtship of Tim and Julianne until it led to their nuptials in St. Martin-in-the-Fields Church in the fall of 1868, just four months after Tim's graduation from medical school.

Scrooge's declining health kept him from attending both events. Instead he remained at home waiting for Tim to visit and share stories of both happy days. After the graduation, Scrooge and Tim shared an intimate moment.

"I don't know how to begin to thank you for the gift of my education," Tim whispered while fighting back his emotions. Tim's unsteadiness evoked sublime pride in Scrooge. The newly minted doctor wore his Kelly green academic hood for Scrooge. He stood from his chair and swirled around modeling it with a healthy balance of pride and humility. Scrooge's applause was intended to thank

Tim for sharing this piece of his graduation from medical school that "Uncle Ebenezer" had missed.

Scrooge surprised Tim with a ready-made reply.

"You have already thanked me by graduating with honors. Now I would ask that you honor me by being my personal physician. Dr. Wilkins has given me notice that he will retire in three months."

Casting a devilish look in his eyes, Scrooge bantered with Tim about a possible scenario. "I hinted to Dr. Wilkins that if he was looking for someone to inherit his practice, I had just the person in mind."

Pausing long enough to convey a wink at Tim, he continued.

"You'll be pleased to know that he is expecting you to contact him."

Tim flashed a smile at Scrooge and said, "Thanks Uncle, for both the reference and recommendation." They shared a glass of port with few words passed between them. The moment was intended to reverence the warmth and depth of their bonds and not chatter about their thoughts.

Before departing, Tim took Scrooge's blood pressure and pulse rate.

"So, Doctor, how much time do you think I have?" Scrooge asked rhetorically.

As Tim placed his pocket watch inside his vest, he harnessed his skillful bedside manners and replied, "I can safely say that you have time to enjoy many more bottles of your favorite port."

They each laughed heartily until Scrooge commanded the last word. "In that case, shall we drink one more glass before you go?"

Tim continued the banter. "Let's make it three glasses if I may invite my wife, Julianne, who has been waiting in the parlor downstairs."

Instead of a farewell handshake, Tim gently placed his right hand on Scrooge's head in a gesture of blessing. Julianne assumed a prayerful posture. The sixty-eight year old patient closed his eyes and breathed in as much of Tim's healing presence as possible. It invigorated him enough to enjoy the freshly baked bread and chicken broth Mrs. Dilber had prepared for his dinner.

Dr. and Mrs. Tim Cratchit left Scrooge's home as quietly as they entered. Tim's heart was torn knowing that those chapters of his life that included Uncle Ebenezer were about to end; but the chapters including his new wife, new profession and, hopefully, a new family, were just about to be written.

Tim and Julianne quickened their steps as they walked toward Kensington Gardens. Both of them somehow knew their hearts were beating in unison with the same dreams and hopes. Before long, their happy musings would turn to sadness.

CHAPTER 14

Martha & Abner

*M*artha's first store was a success. She trademarked the name "Hats and
Hello's." The "Hat's" piece highlighted her classy merchandise. The
"Hello's" piece was the tea, coffee and biscuits room where customers lingered
and chatted about how women could better resolve England's problems if only
asked by the men. Her vision of twinning goods, then lingering for conversation with other customers was an idea ahead of its time.

She traveled to Europe three times a year to buy the latest couture chapeaux's
for her burgeoning high society clientele. At Scrooge's suggestion she began stocking special items for men, the breed of gentlemen with fine taste for fine attire.

Three years after opening her first store on Bond Street she discussed with
Scrooge the idea of expanding with a second store on fashionable Oxford Street.
True to his word, he advanced her the interest portion of the loan she had repaid
in record time. It was enough to buy a corner store. Martha looked upon that
property as the doorway to the Promised Land.

While expanding and sharpening her business skills, her relationship with
Abner Solomon was becoming complicated. In hindsight, Peter's suspicions
were surfacing. Abner wanted more of her time, attention and, ultimately,
her good fortune. Abner, resigned to simply clerking at his father's accounting
firm, grew more resentful of Martha's independence and success. His misery was fueled by jealousy of her relationship with the prominent Ebenezer
Scrooge. Abner's bitterness was rooted in his absence of a wealthy patron who
could be the architect of a path to becoming a man of independent means, a role
that Scrooge was playing for Martha.

One evening, while dining at Martha's house, Abner waited for her parents
to leave before unleashing his pent-up anger.

"I never see you much anymore. We never go out for dinner or to the theatre or just for a walk in Hyde Park or window shop along Oxford Street."

Martha watched the veins in Abner's neck stiffen as he increased his display of anger.

"Have you replaced me with your hats and customers?" he shouted sarcastically while pouring another glass of wine to fortify his aggressiveness.

She kept her composure while steeling herself for his oncoming volleys.

"You rejected my application as accountant for your business, leaving me to the humiliation of working for my condescending father."

Martha stole the moment to speak while he drank a full glass of wine.

"Is this your agenda - the fact that I would not hire you? Is this what your un-gentlemanly behavior is all about?

"Hell no, it's about feeling rejected by someone who I thought had feelings for me."

"Right now I would say you're not doing a very good job convincing me about the honest nature of those feelings," Martha easily matched his bravado.

She watched as his eyes tightened and his face twisted into someone sinister.

"Do we have a future or not?" Abner yelled as he spiraled into intoxication.

Controlling her emotions, she stood from her place at the table and spoke calmly, but deliberately. "I don't know about a future, Abner, but as far as tonight I am sure it's time for you to leave."

Abner rose from his place opposite Martha, and on a quick impulse, reached over and slapped her so hard across the face that she fell back against the dining room wall. As he rounded the table to physically attack her again, she raised her right hand and pulled the bell chord. In less than ten seconds, her housemaid, Janet, entered through the butler's pantry. She moved quickly to Martha's aid.

"Are you all right, Miss Cratchit?" She buttressed herself between Martha and Abner.

With her lower lip, swollen and bleeding, Martha felt energized to stand. While facing Abner just a few feet away, she defiantly ended their confrontation. "Mr. Solomon is leaving. Please show him to the door."

Abner Solomon took a moment to process Martha's words. With Janet as a potential witness, he thought it best to exit. Following Janet to the hallway, he gathered his cape, hat and gloves, and left wondering what the next chapter in this scenario would be. Martha knew that he would never be invited back.

The next day Martha sent a note to her manager at the Bond Street Store that she was taking a few days off to ponder details about the new Oxford Street store. Knowing her business was in good hands, she sent a note to her mother asking if she could stay at the *Clift Side* cottage for a few days of rest. When a courier delivered the affirmative reply, Martha packed a bag, took a taxi to Charing Cross Rail Station and headed for Dover.

Unbeknownst to her, Alice Cratchit had sent a cable alerting Magdalena McCready that her daughter Martha was en route to the cottage for a few days. Martha had hoped that the pleasant change of scenery, along with the crisp ocean air would calm her frayed emotions and heal the ugly bruise festering on her lower lip. While that was happening she vowed to purge Abner Solomon from her life.

Halfway into the second day of her respite, Martha received a cable from her parents that the Oxford Street store, which was being cleaned and prepared for renovation, had caught fire. Sadly, the damage was extensive. While the sky was crystal clear in Dover, Martha felt the shadows of dark clouds circling her like an impending storm. She would stay one more day for clarity on what she had to do upon her return.

CHAPTER 15

Scrooge & Martha

Two days after returning from Dover, Martha met with insurance adjustors to discuss claims against the charred property at Oxford Street. Fire inspectors had concluded that the blaze, linked with flammable cleaning solvents, was incendiary in nature. This left everyone thinking criminal activity without anyone speaking those horrifying words.

Fifteen minutes after her meeting Martha raised the brass door knocker at Scrooge's house in Mayfair and waited for Mrs. Dilber to answer.

Scrooge, who was seated in his library reading a book of Elizabeth Barrett Browning poetry, greeted her with a genuine hug followed by words of sympathy and concern regarding the fire.

"That's why I am here, Uncle Ebenezer," Martha said in a steady voice. Scrooge studied the partially healed cut on her lip and the near-fading bruise. Cosmetics could not completely hide the obvious. He suspected that a story to her appearance was linked with the fire. Walking with her to a nearby sofa, Scrooge thought it best to let her share the details.

"I just came from meeting with fire inspectors at Oxford Street. The evidence proves it was not accidental." She paused long enough for Scrooge to absorb the import of her statement.

What she said next rattled Scrooge. "I have reason to believe that Abner Solomon caused that fire. Last week he attacked and wounded me after dinner at my house. If it hadn't been for Janet coming to my aid, he might have injured me far worse than this."

"Abner left filled with rage and scorn, feeling that I rejected him. Underneath his charming persona, is a villain in disguise. The fire was his revenge. I have no evidence, just sure feelings."

Looking straight at Scrooge, she spoke words he didn't want to hear.

"I fear he is capable of setting the Bond Street store on fire also, and I need your help in thwarting that."

"I'm listening."

"Do you know anyone who could guard the store from the inside and catch him in the act, if possible?"

Scrooge reached out and clasped Martha's hands. Then, with all the assurance he could muster, said calmly,

"I do. Let me take care of this. You have enough to worry about."

"One last thing, Uncle," Martha said while tightening her grip on his hands, "can we keep this conversation between the two of us?"

Scrooge's firm headshake was the answer she needed.

She stayed awhile and shared some details about her retreat at the Dover cottage. They hugged warmly at the door. Scrooge waved as the taxi whisked her away.

Returning to the library, he immediately sat at his desk and wrote a confidential note to Chief Inspector Arthur Mulberry at Scotland Yard. He sent it by courier and knew that the veteran detective would pay him a visit quickly.

CHAPTER 16

Scrooge & Inspector Mulberry

*I*n less than three hours after receiving his note, Chief Inspector Mulberry was sitting in Scrooge's library, taking detailed notes as Scrooge shared the specifics of his plan.

"Just to be clear Mr. Scrooge, you are asking my help in securing Miss Cratchit's store on Bond Street because she fears a repeat of what happened to the store on Oxford Street. Is that correct?"

"Yes Inspector, that is correct," Scrooge answered succinctly.

"I have a friend, Mr. Brian Weller, trained at Scotland Yard, who now owns a security agency. He is licensed to carry a weapon. With your permission I will contact him and ask if he is available for this assignment. He can protect the property from the inside. I can assign a police detail to regularly patrol the outside."

"You may assume that permission, Inspector, and ask him to send his bill to my address." Scrooge hesitated momentarily then added, "If there is a paper trail I want it to lead to me and not to my niece."

The Chief Inspector agreed. "That is prudent considering her delicate situation as a female business owner. If Brian Weller is available, I will arrange to bring him here so the two of you can meet."

They parted at the front door with a firm handshake. The next day Inspector Mulberry notified Scrooge that Brian had accepted the assignment.

They arrived shortly after Martha and Scrooge had finished lunch. The veteran Scotland Yard Chief Inspector wanted her present for this meeting. The differences in the two men were glaring. Inspector Mulberry emitted a gruff persuasion as a well-respected detective thriving on fighting crime. But, Martha was bewitched by Brian Weller. His pretty boy good looks provided a natural decoy for being aggressive and diligent in protecting people's rights and property. Anticipating this meeting, Scrooge had his solicitor draft a contract stipulating the terms of Brian Weller's employment and salary.

As the handsome professional was reading the fine print, Martha studied Brian's stature and felt an attraction to his features and manners. She registered an impulse of comfort in his carriage and demeanor that gave her a sense of confidence that her store would be in good hands from the time she closed at 6:00 pm and opened again at 9:00 am. She felt assured that Brian Weller was the right man to confront Abner Solomon in the event he foolishly tried to exact further revenge.

After he signed the contract, Martha initiated a conversation.

"Mr. Weller, if you come by the store tomorrow I can show you the floor plan, particularly the office space you may use to camouflage your presence during the night. You will be happy to know that there is indoor plumbing for your convenience."

"Thank you, would 1:00 pm tomorrow be convenient," Brian asked sounding more charming than professional. "Also, is there a rear entrance, Miss Cratchit?"

"Yes sir," Martha answered then added, "Is that important?"

"Yes, Miss and I will explain why tomorrow."

While Mrs. Dilber showed the gentlemen out, Scrooge and Martha chatted briefly. As a pseudo-business partner, Scrooge assured her that this course of action was necessary to relieve her stress and hopefully, in time, catch the arsonist red-handed.

The next day Brian was punctual. Martha gave him a tour of the two-story building in a casual manner, not wanting to fuel attention or panic among her sales staff or customers. Back in the office, Brian fortified her assurance that he could be trusted to keep her property safe.

Behind his good looks and allurements, she noticed a smart and attentive security professional. He had an odd trusting streak and to her dismay, she enjoyed how it stirred some unexpected romantic urges in her.

"Keep this professional," she told herself quietly. She waited for a reply from her conscience that never came.

With a mixture of curiosity and desire, Martha initiated a conversation. "Mr. Weller, are you inclined to share with me some of the ideas you have for protecting my store?"

"Since we may be dealing with potential criminal activity, Miss Cratchit, I think it best to keep details confidential for now." Martha gestured with a slight bow of her head.

Brian's tactics for securing the store were simple, but effective. He used a telescope to monitor movement and activity outside on Bond Street from a second floor window. He moved around the store in stocking feet to muffle any sound. He installed a dead bolt device on both doors making it difficult for an intruder to enter without noise. Brian attached a bell on the rear door that rang when it opened. Finally, with the help of Inspector Mulberry, police were alerted to his presence inside and were positioned close by in case he needed them.

On the fourth night of his surveillance Brian's skills paid off. At 2:30 am an intruder broke a glass pane on the rear door. While trying to dislodge the special lock, the bell chimed. Brian lit a small lamp in the second floor front window. It was a signal to the police. He quickly crept back to the stairway landing, affording him a direct view of the intruder once he got inside.

Brian, with revolver drawn, saw a shadow. The intruder had stepped inside then quickly struck a match to a flammable device. As he prepared to throw it further inside the store, Brian yelled, "Don't move or I'll shoot." Shocked by the sound of an unexpected voice in the dead of night, Abner dropped the incendiary which quickly ignited with the carpet and flared up, caused by a swift backdraft from the open door, catching hold of his trousers. Feeling both of his legs on fire, Abner turned to flee. But Brian's gun was faster. One shot struck Abner in the torso. He dropped to the floor. By the time Brian approached, he was dead. Brian quickly located a bucket of water in a nearby closet to douse the flames engulfing Abner.

Police whistles sounded and before long a small army arrived, including two Bobbies, who helped Brian extinguish the fire before it spread. The damage was minimal, but the store became a crime scene with the arsonist partially charred. After identifying his body, Martha closed it for two days while the police and forensic specialists helped to bring this nightmare to a close.

On the day the store reopened, Brian Weller paid a visit and purchased an expensive cravat. Charmed by his appearance, Martha surrendered to a playful instinct.

"Mr. Weller, that cravat needs an equally attractive stickpin. Allow me to pick it out as a gift from a grateful shop owner."

They talked in her office for over an hour, which included making plans for dinner.

"Do you have a favorite restaurant, Miss Cratchit?

Martha teased Brian until they both were smiling.

"I have many favorite restaurants, Mr. Weller. You're welcome to surprise me until the list gets short."

CHAPTER 17

Peter & Abigail

*E*xactly nine months after their playful and passionate lovemaking week-end at the cottage, Abigail gave birth to twin girls. Named Amanda and Priscilla, on the day of their baptism, Peter teased his adoring wife about their double portion of good fortune.

"It's a good thing we didn't stay three days at the cottage or the twins might have been triplets."

They giggled together as a way of playfully honoring their miracle. As Abigail mothered the girls, Peter spent more time with four-year old Victor. The following winter the young boy's health took an alarming turn. Tim was summoned from medical school.

The symptoms of a high fever, a swollen tongue and a fast spreading sand-paper pink rash on Victor's chest meant only one thing. Tim called in Dr. Manette for a consult. After the examination they spoke clearly with their eyes only. The doctor's slight bow of the head was a pre-arranged signal of confirm-ing the diagnosis. Tim asked Peter and Abigail to step outside the bedroom.

In an unsteady voice, he spoke the words they did not want to hear.

"I'm sorry to tell you that the symptoms clearly indicate scarlet fever."

Peter embraced his wife to keep her from collapsing. She wept profusely. Peter joined his tears with hers while Tim stood close by feeling helpless.

In a voice of desperation, Peter asked Tim, "Please help him so he's not in pain."

"The incubation period is usually one to seven days. His undeveloped immune system, unfortunately, will not help him. Forgive me for sounding so clinical, Peter."

Reaching out and placing his hand on his brother's shoulder, Tim became consoling. "As your brother, I am so sorry for you and Abby."

Two days later Victor's breathing became sporadic. Tim stayed close to his bedside, trying to provide him whatever comfort he could. The Vicar of St. Justin's Church was called for anointing. Each Cratchit and Langley took turns watching over the boy while flooding heaven with prayers for a miracle.

Shortly after midnight on the third day Victor drew his last breath and expired peacefully. Tim felt for a pulse and continued holding his nephew's wrist until Alice joined her hand to his and eventually, helped him to let go.

Peter and Abigail, though surrounded with the most abundant love and comfort from both families, were devastated. Martha visited Scrooge later in the morning to share the sad news in person. They wept together with Scrooge's tears seeming heavier because of the mystery of one so young being taken before Scrooge, who, at sixty-nine had lived a full and contented life.

"I wish it could have been me. His life was just beginning, and I will miss not getting to know him." Scrooge mused almost mournfully.

"Martha, please convey my sorrow and sympathies to Peter and Abigail and let me know what comfort I can offer as your uncle." Those words from Scrooge stirred more tears from Martha. She reached over and hugged him again for a second dose of comfort.

Following Victor's burial rites, the Cratchit's and the Langley's took turns caring for Amanda and Priscilla while Peter and his broken-hearted wife went to the cottage for some much needed rest and healing.

They stood, hand-in-hand, along the white cliffs each day and watched the sea beat along the shoreline. As they absorbed the rhythm of the ebb and flow of the ocean it burst the damn of their broken hearts and began to melt their pain. Gradually they surrendered their son to the eternal care of the God who gave him life. The wideness of the ocean awakened them to a blessed assurance that God's arms were wide enough to embrace them and gather their pain into his arms. Before they returned to London, they committed themselves to focus on the living and renewed their vows to parent their girls as devoted mother and father.

They ended their retreat with subdued lovemaking. They fell asleep in each other's arms, but not before uttering a prayer that the cottage would work its magic again, and the creator God who dwells there in wondrous and mysterious ways would bless them with another child.

CHAPTER 18

Tim & Julianne

*T*he Cratchit family grieved for nearly a year following Victor's death. During this time, Tim began a prolonged contemplation of a deep desire for children. Sharing it with his wife, Julianne surprised him by sharing the same desire. They agreed to begin planning for a family. As time passed, with no promising results, Tim decided to examine his sperm in the university surgical lab. The results confirmed his suspicions. It pained him to share with Julianne that she had some physical impediment for conceiving. Hoping her medical condition was temporary they decided to adopt a child from an orphanage.

With Christmas fast approaching they put the adoption on hold until after the holidays. Scrooge's health was failing and Tim needed to be available for any emergency. Also, if adoption was on the horizon after the New Year, Julianne needed to give notice at the hospital of her departure from the surgical staff.

In the meantime, they shared with Tim's parents their plans for adoption. Bob and Alice, as expected, were thoroughly supportive.

"May I suggest you visit Mr. Scrooge's orphanage, Holy Child House, in the East End." Alice let her words settle quietly in the couple's mind and hearts.

Wearing a soft smile, Tim replied, "Thank you Mama, for that suggestion. We will consider it."

Bob then took command of the conversation.

"Tim and Julianne, Alice and I have been talking about gathering the family together for Christmas at the cottage. It has been a sad year for all of us, especially Peter and Abigail and Martha. We would like to know your thoughts."

The four of them chatted enthusiastically about the idea. Tim placed reservations on his attendance for a three-day holiday because of Scrooge's health. "I would have to be ready to return via the train at a moment's notice if he turns critical."

As the holidays approached Tim's surgical practice became more demanding. Sometimes he operated with Julianne on the surgical team. Having her by his side generated pleasant moments for both.

For some time, Tim had been researching traction and splinting procedures developed by a physician in Liverpool. Dr. Hugh Thomas, a distinguished Alumni of University College, had fine-tuned the medical art of bone-setting. Intrigued by his findings, Tim yearned to meet Dr. Thomas in person, and hoped that such a renowned colleague could guide him in his interest in orthopedic surgery. During dinner one evening Tim discussed the subject with Julianne. He opened his heart to her for the first time on the subject of his spinal difficulties during childhood.

"Julianne, I never shared with you that I was born with a spinal abnormality. It interfered with my schooling, forcing me to study at home. Unlike other children in the neighborhood I wasn't able to play sports. Thanks to a tutor I became a respectable Chess player."

His wife glued her eyes on Tim. They spoke care and attention to him. She thought she knew everything about Tim, but Julianne was hearing things for the first time. His fragility inspired her to reach over and hold his hand. He drew a deep breath and continued.

"When I was fourteen, I traveled to Europe with my parents to receive a new experimental traction procedure developed by a Belgium military surgeon."

"That orthopedic method was a risk that changed my life. I will forever be indebted to that surgeon and to Uncle Ebenezer for funding the trip and my treatment." Tim's voice grew unsteady as he expressed his gratitude.

Julianne held Tim's hands tightly with hers as she gathered her thoughts.

"I was unaware of this chapter in your life. Thank you for sharing it. It gives me clarity on your plans. Is there anything else you wish to tell me?"

"I am ready to contract Dr. Thomas and arrange a visit."

"If that will make you happy dear, I will help you prepare for your trip."

"Actually, I was hoping you would join me," Tim replied, catching his wife by surprise.

"I could use your opinion and insights about the doctor's character and procedures. You are, after all a nurse and the daughter of a respected surgeon." Tim's flattery was intended as leverage to persuade Julianne to join him.

They traveled by train to Liverpool and spent two days observing Dr. Thomas's bone-setting practices at his clinic. While Tim was greatly enthused by what he saw, Julianne had reservations.

During the return trip to London, she shared her critique of Dr. Thomas as being an irascible and temperamental man. Short of stature and harsh in his words, Julianne sarcastically remarked that he flunked the course on bedside manners in medical school.

"However, after watching his skills and seeing the results, if I had to decide between surgery and pain, I would risk surgery," she said wearing a serious expression on her face.

Not wanting to antagonize her accurate description of Dr. Thomas's personality, Tim's focus was different.

"I was able to transcend his human flaws to learn his skillful art of bone-setting. And when it comes to bedside manners, my dear, you are spoiled by a father and a husband who lavish you with good manners." Tim added a distinct wink hoping to smooth his wife's mood. As always it worked. Julianne leaned over and planted an endearing kiss on his face.

Tim returned north and spent a month observing and assisting Dr. Thomas. He returned home with crystal clarity on an inner call to make orthopedic surgery his specialty.

He began operating on the fractured bones of children with stunning success. The more children healed with broken femurs and arms, he developed a fondness for children with bone impediments. He vividly recalled the chapters in his life when he was one of them and began to entertain a thought of adopting such a child as a parent.

Julianne shared the same feelings. It's what drew them to Holy Child Orphanage. There they found a ten-month old boy born with a severe bone deformity in both legs. Before departing they signed papers expressing interest in his adoption. Four weeks later they returned and left with their new son, Owen Cratchit.

Though he was not a physically perfect child, his adoption was not motivated by his flawless exterior features, but by his adopted parents' desire to discover new ways to love and nurture him to live a full life beyond his impediments.

For Tim and Julianne, this was the ultimate test of true parenthood and they committed themselves to practicing it with the utmost devotion.

CHAPTER 19

Martha Cratchit & Brian Weller

*B*rian Weller was everything Abner Solomon was not. He was an atypical Victorian male who did not subscribe to the mentality that women should be submissive to men. Brian was comfortable with Martha's status as a successful business woman. He had a steady temperament and was not prone to violence. He had a healthy sense of humor and enjoyed teasing Martha as much as he listened to her talk about ladies apparel. He could wine and dine her on Saturday nights, then accompany her to church on Sunday morning. They could talk about their businesses as pleasantly as they talked about their growing fondness for each other. Finally, Brian was patient in their courtship, without releasing the tension of unmet expectations. All of these qualities mattered to Martha.

Six months after the arson nightmare with Abner Solomon, Brian had become Martha's miracle worker. His charm and solicitations worked a magic on her. In record time, her hope was renewed about the joy of becoming Brian's wife.

One of their most enjoyable outings was a tour of Scotland Yard. Brian used his influence to give Martha a private look at the inner labyrinth of London's famous police center. She was surprised to learn that the address of the Metropolitan Police Headquarters, located at 4 Whitehall Place, had a rear entrance to a street called, 'Great Scotland Yard.' Brian winked hoping Martha would solve the puzzle.

"I often wondered what connection Scotland had with London's police headquarters," Martha said amusingly. "And here I find out it is a street and not the country." These pleasant forays bonded their ties for each other in a way that deepened their mutual affections.

As the seasons of the year changed Martha hoped to find an engagement ring hidden in her stocking on Christmas Day. She controlled her naturally extroverted inclination and kept that desire to herself. Martha did not wish to sabotage an enduring relationship with Brian by second guessing his heart.

A week before Christmas, during dinner at Mansfield House, Brian surprised Martha with a question.

"Can you give me a hint of what gift I can give you for Christmas?"

Her emotions swung from surprise to pondering. She wasn't sure if he was serious or tormenting her, so Martha decided to take the high road of playful discretion.

"Well Brian, you know me well enough to know what my desires are."

While curling his lips into a teasing smile and raising his eyebrows for visual effect, Brian matched Martha's innuendo with his reply.

"It's a good thing for you that I am a master at solving riddles."

All Martha could do was wink and hope that Brian got the message. After dinner they attended a performance of the play, "The Frozen Deep" at the St. James Theatre. Seated in a loge box was the famed author Charles Dickens. Martha raised an eyebrow knowing that the female seated with him was not his wife, Catherine. Martha had heard rumors about the author's clandestine affair with a younger woman and wondered if the one accompanying Dickens that evening was his new 'Mistress.'

Later as they waited in line for a carriage, Martha warmed her frozen hands by burying them deeper into Brian's arm. She hoped that he could imagine how a certain finger on her left hand would be much warmer and brighter.

CHAPTER 20

Christmas at Dover Cottage – 1870

*A*lice Cratchit was a master at planning family events. Hosting the family for a three-day Christmas gathering at the Dover cottage was a task that energized her. She solicited Bob's help immediately.

Previous holidays found their children sneaking into their parent's home at different times during Christmas Day, and always with the disappointment of departing early to visit in-laws. Also, their brief, but pleasant visits to Uncle Scrooge kept his spirits up. Each of them knew that hearing as many "Merry Christmases" as possible made his heart full and his soul dance.

Now that grandchildren were in the picture Alice quietly harbored a plan to make the family holiday trip to Dover an annual tradition. She shared this dream with Bob only.

"To ensure this becomes an annual tradition, my dear Robert, I propose we pay for everyone's train fare to and from Dover." She spoke her line nonchalantly as she stitched some final touches to new dresses for her twin granddaughters for Christmas.

Bob continued reading the evening newspaper, but mollified her with a comment, "Whatever you say my dear. Just let me know in advance what bank I need to rob." He lowered the newspaper to see her flashing a smile that was "a la" Alice Cratchit. He flashed one back to her. In these most endearing moments they spoke, 'I love you,' with their eyes only.

As the senior partner at Scrooge & Cratchit, Bob's income had enabled them to move from Camden Town to a three-story home in the Brompton area of London. He lightened his wife's domestic load by hiring a fulltime house-maid and cook, and when they entertained high society investors, he brought in a butler and a footman for dinner parties. They continued chatting, both on the same page but focused on different things.

CHAPTER 21

Tim & Scrooge

T wo days before the family gathering Tim visited Scrooge to check on his health and share some early Christmas merriment.

"Don't fret about me while you are in Dover. Enjoy the change of scenery with your family. I'm in good hands with Mrs. Dilber and her niece nursing me. I will wait to hear your stories upon your return."

Before he left, they exchanged the same gifts they have given the past ten years. Tim handed Scrooge a bottle of his favorite Portuguese wine wrapped with a red and green ribbon. Scrooge reciprocated with a renewed membership to his City Gentlemen's Club. The humble, but gracious doctor only used it when entertaining physicians visiting London.

"I have left clear instructions with Mrs. Dilber how to contact Dr. Manette in the event of an emergency." Tim assured his uncle that he had not overlooked any detail.

Before leaving Scrooge's house, Tim placed a new ornament on the six foot Frazer fir that adorned his parlor. He knew Scrooge would muse about it during his next visit. Before arriving at home, he visited a store to buy several Christmas toys for Owen. His one-year old son would soon need toys to distract him after Tim finished a series of surgeries to correct the boy's crippled legs.

Owen was delighted with his father's choices, and Julianne gave her husband an affectionate hug for his thoughtfulness. They were ideal parents for a one-year old son who, in spite of his disability, was treated no differently than any other child.

Owen brought a sense of fulfillment to his parent's lives and the three bonded together as intimately as the Holy Trinity. Tim and Julianne had already decided that after Owen's surgery and recovery they would adopt a second child, for their threesome was overflowing with love.

CHAPTER 22

*T*he entire family, including Brian Weller, gathered at Charing Cross Station to travel together on the same train to Dover. Oliver McCready had arranged for three carriages to bring them to the cottage upon their arrival. Alice, sensitive about the issue of her twin granddaughters visiting Dover cottage for the first time, discussed the issue with Oliver and Magdalena.

"Mr. Cratchit and I certainly feel that you are part of our family. We value the way you care for our cottage and trust you like we do our children, but if the visit of the twin girls is the cause of any discomfort or sadness, then please feel free to take a holiday when the family visits."

The middle-aged couple anticipated the discussion. Magdalena deferred to Oliver in expressing their sentiments.

"Thank you Mrs. Cratchit for the delicate way you have respected us and our broken hearts. We appreciate the choice you and Mr. Cratchit have offered, but we have decided to remain here. Celebrating with your family will rescue us from the sadness of spending another Christmas alone. Being of help to you, trimming the tree and preparing the meals will lift our spirits and give us cause to feel blessed beyond our loss.

Alice contained her emotions while expressing her delight.

"I am pleased that you have chosen to join us. The children will be enchanted by your company, and of course, I will be grateful for your help. We will make the holidays as memorable as possible."

By the time everyone had arrived at the cottage, Oliver had warm fires brewing in all six fireplaces. He greeted everyone at the door while Magdalena gathered their coats and scarves and neatly placed them on a rack in the hallway. Peter and Abigail, alive to their raw feelings about twin girls, introduced the couple to Amanda and Priscilla. Their unsteadiness passed quickly as Abigail handed each of the devoted caretakers one of their girls. The McCready's cuddled them tightly as tears streamed down their faces. The sacredness of the moment was hallowed by unhinged emotions and reverent silence.

CHAPTER 23

Christmas Eve day was full of frenzy and activity. Oliver had secured a five-foot spruce tree neatly into a parlor corner. Alice had brought her collection of cherished ornaments and decorations on previous trips from London.

While she and Magdalena busied themselves with breakfast in the kitchen, the rest of the family went to work trimming the house with Christmas cheer. As they pieced together garlands of trinkets to hang over mantelpieces and the main stairway, others decorated the tree. All joined in singing traditional carols; "Good King Wenceslaus," "God Rest Ye Merry Gentlemen," "The Sussex Carol," and "I Heard the Bells on Christmas Day." The last selection was a family favorite with the words written by Henry Wadsworth Longfellow.

With sixteen hands committed to decorating, they finished in record time. A silence pervaded the house as the family began writing Christmas cards to stuff in stockings.

In the kitchen, Alice was hard at work making mince pies for dessert after the Christmas Eve church service, while Magdalena prepared chestnut stuffing for the turkey. The last chore in the morning for Alice was mixing her famous plum pudding, the family's traditional dessert on Christmas Day.

Martha and Brian set the table for the ten adults and three children.

"I never imagined the cottage being this enchanting," Brian said as he neatly arranged place settings and stemware.

"It has been special to my parents ever since they honeymooned here. They have celebrated every anniversary here since." Martha spoke with warm affection for what had become known as the family "country home."

"My father's promotion came at the same time the cottage was for sale. It was fortuitous that they were able to purchase it."

Then she assumed a teasing attitude toward Brian.

"Maybe someday we will have fond memories of *Clift Side Cottage* as my parents have."

Brian astonished her with his reply.

"Or we just might start a new set of memories in our own cottage." That line left her mute - not a characteristic behavior for Martha Cratchit. The best she could do was flash a genuine smile, while her heart pulsed with high expectation for a certain Christmas gift.

They attended the 6:00 pm Christmas Eve Vigil service at St. Mary of the Virgin Church. The choir sang a moving rendition of "The Coventry Carol," and two hundred voices in attendance shook the church rafters with the hymn, "The First Noel."

Back in the cottage by 7:30 pm, Magdalena served warm mince pies, coffee and tea.

After Christmas stockings were placed underneath the tree, everyone retired for the night. Everyone, except Bob and Alice.

They quietly returned to the parlor, lit a gas lamp and sat arm-in-arm on the sofa, each holding a glass of brandy.

"After thirty-five years of marriage, this is the best Christmas ever Robert," Alice pined softly.

"Yes, my dear, who would have ever thought we would be this fortunate? We owe much of this to Mr. Scrooge. After the New Year, I must begin to discuss with him how we might best honor his legacy."

They rested in each other's arms, enchanted by the sparkle of the tree ornaments reflected by the gas lamp. Each gave silent thanks for the blessings they had received over the years. When their brandy glasses were empty, they slowly retired up the stairs holding hands.

CHAPTER 24

Christmas Day at the Cottage

The twin girls and young Owen Cratchit were the first to wake. Soon everyone gathered in the parlor to share Christmas stockings and exchange cards.

Everyone's attention focused on the three children. Their kiddy talk, coupled with delight in their eyes and smiles on their faces were better than any poor attempt to speak well-formulated words.

As for the adults, oohs and aahs and hugs were the typical responses to the gift giving. Martha emptied her stocking without the gift she expected. Brian studied her reactions, and to his delight, she withheld expressing the slightest hint of disappointment. It affirmed her sterling character and assured him of his true love for her. He had something more surprising planned later that day.

They ate a hearty breakfast, then, with the McCready's as nursemaids, the adults strolled around the edge of the cliffs. Peter and Abigail held hands tightly as they reminisced about the walks they took not too long ago to heal their grief over Victor's death. They treasured those memories quietly in their hearts. Thanks to the blessing of Amanda and Priscilla, the sadness over the death of their son ended with a double portion of joy by parenting two beautiful daughters.

Tim and Julianne chatted quietly about a second adoption after the New Year. Martha and Brian walked arm in arm breathing in the salt air and reflected on the new memories of this first Christmas in each other's lives.

Bob and Alice lingered behind to privately reminisce and smile about their wonderful growing family.

"I can't ever remember being happier than I am today, Robert."

"I share your sentiment my dear, and swell with joy at the hope that we will soon relocate here and grow old together."

Back in the cottage the aroma of a Christmas feast was wafting through the house.

They enjoyed cordials and appetizers in the parlor. As the grandfather clock on the stairway landing struck 6:00 pm, with the sun set beyond the most western cliff, they moved to the dining room for dinner.

Magdalena had outdone herself decorating the table with a garland of sprigs and cinnamon sticks. A large vase of holly and evergreen branches accented the sideboard. In the center a ribbon of pine cones encircled a gingerbread house which charmed the children. Candles on the table added a romantic glow to the occasion. At each place setting a peppermint stick had been neatly placed in the napkin rings. These personal touches were created by Magdalena as gifts to the Cratchits from her and Oliver.

Standing at their places, Robert offered a table prayer echoing the shared sentiments for the blessing of their Christmas gathering. Then the feasting began.

Bob carved the turkey and placed a generous serving on each plate alongside with a scoop of chestnut stuffing. Brussels sprouts and potatoes in butter with fresh parsley were served family style along with Yorkshire pudding. Wine flowed abundantly, spiking the chatter with storied laughter.

The family lingered at the table long after Magdalena and Oliver had cleared the dishes. Then an annual ritual began as Peter, the oldest child, paraded into the dining room presenting Alice's famed plum pudding in a silver bowl.

Then Martha poured brandy over the pudding while Tim struck a match setting the traditional dessert aflame. This ritual was performed with precision as if they were lighting gas lamps in the town square.

This time-honored Christmas dessert ritual contained a much anticipated surprise. For whoever found the silver Christmas tree charm baked into the pudding could count on an abundance of good luck in the New Year. For this reason, the pudding was eaten slowly, not only to savor its delicious sweetness, but in the hopes of finding the cherished silver charm.

This year, Alice consented to a special request from Brian Weller. Alice assured Brain that he would receive a certain portion of the pudding. Once he discovered the "charm", he dipped it into his water glass, dried it with his napkin, got on one knee next to Martha and said,

"My one and only Martha, I won't take 'No" for an answer as I ask you to marry me."

She spoke as if she had rehearsed her line for months. "In that case, my one and only Brian, 'yes, yes, a thousand times yes.'"

While the newly engaged couple shared a long hug, everyone else clapped their approval, while some wiped away their tears. Bob raised his wine glass. The rest of the family joined in the gesture.

"Brian, Alice and I couldn't be happier having you as a son-in-law. Let's drink a toast to the newly engaged couple."

The taste of the brandy lingered on everyone's palate long after the pudding had been consumed. After the children had been put to bed, the adults gathered in the parlor to share memories of their first Christmas in Dover, and to make plans for a revered and traditional Boxing Day outing.

CHAPTER 25

Boxing Day – 1870

*I*n this family, Boxing Day carried a hallowed mystique. Every December 26th the Cratchits joined their fellow Brits in filling alms boxes and distributing them to the poor. Once the boxes were filled, the Cratchits divided into three groups. Peter & Abigail along with Martha & Brian headed for the Mercy House at the ferry port. Bob & Alice along with Oliver & Magdalena headed for the hospital. Tim & Julianne went to visit the orphanage. Each of them carried a box filled with Christmas cookies and treats and, for the adults, a pair of gloves, a scarf and cap for the winter. The scarves, one dozen of them, had been crocheted by the caring hands of Alice Cratchit.

At the hospital, Bob & Alice, Oliver & Magdalena separated to visit the maximum number of patients. The McCready's had been regular visitors ever since Alice practiced her special brand of caregiving and rescued them in the same hospital. They chatted briefly with patients, especially those who had no visitors, and left alms boxes wrapped in Christmas ribbons and adorned with a sprig of holly.

At the orphanage, Tim & Julianne, with Owen in a baby carriage, entertained children in a nursery room. They handed out toys which delighted the children, along with a peppermint stick.

Tim and Julianne were drawn to a young six-month old girl named Sophie, who had arrived at the orphanage one week earlier. She stiffened her body at the sight of them and extended her arms from the crib as if to say, "Please hold me." So pleasant was her disposition that they held her smile for a long time in their hearts. Their eyes danced between Sophie and one another. They each knew what the other was thinking. Before they departed, Tim and Julianne spoke with the director about possibly adopting Sophie after the New Year. She agreed to begin the paper work and to schedule a meeting with them in about a month's time.

Down at the ferry port, Peter & Abigail, along with Martha & Brian visited with some immigrants seeking asylum in England.

Brian and Martha encountered a man from Ireland.

He introduced himself as Mr. Liam Finley. He was thin as a rail and unshaven. His facial appearance was all the more blighted by a set of bad teeth. The soles of his shoes were worn through and his socks were in bad need of some darning by Alice Cratchit. Yet, in spite of his physical appearance, his morale was surprisingly upbeat.

"Mr. Finley, I am Martha Cratchit and this is my fiancé Brian Weller. We have an alms box for you and we would be honored if you accept it." Martha was sensitive in her choice of words.

The disheveled Irishman gave her a pleasant smile. "I do accept it, and, I thank you for your kindness." Then to the couple's astonishment he said, pleadingly,

"And I will accept any work if you have some to offer."

Brian responded with sensitivity.

"What kind of work skills do you have, Mr. Finley?"

"Back in Limerick I was head of maintenance at an iron works factory." Lowering his head and softening his voice, he added, "but as a beggar I am not choosy."

"Mr. Finley, give us some time to discuss this and we promise to get back to you, perhaps later today. Is that agreed?" Brian's words widened Finley's smile. He spoke with an affirming headshake.

After they left the Mercy House, Brian and Martha walked along the Strand and discussed options for Mr. Finley.

Everyone returned to the house for lunch. As they sat down at the table, a cable arrived for Tim. A message from Dr. Manette was clear: *"Mr. Scrooge lapsing into unconsciousness. His passing is imminent."*

Oliver drove Tim to the rail station to catch the next train to London. He arrived at 3:45 pm with little time to spare. Ebenezer Scrooge died at 4:30 pm at the age of seventy, wearing a very serene expression. Tim, Fred, his wife

Catherine, Mrs. Dilber, her niece Colleen and Scrooge's solicitor, Mr. Josiah Benham, remained with the body until the undertaker arrived. During the wait, they each shared colorful stories of their association with the venerable uncle and miser-turned-philanthropist. Occasionally, their chuckles echoed through his well-appointed bedroom.

Fred was the first to speak. "I never thought I would be saying this but, I am going to miss him. I have been so proud to call him 'Uncle' these past twenty years. Now that he is passed I will say, 'Bah Humbug.'" Soft chuckles echoed through the bed chamber.

His wife Catherine shared her own sentiments. "I am glad the children are old enough to have fond memories of him. They will miss the unique ways he cheered them during his Sunday visits."

Mrs. Dilber, with some quivering in her voice, chimed in. "I don't know what I'm going to do now that Mr. Scrooge has passed." Catherine reached out to hold her hand and offer assurance.

"Don't fret about that Mrs. Dilber. Fred and I will welcome you."

Mr. Josiah Benham, the long-time solicitor, was more philosophical in his musings. "It has been such a pleasure providing legal assistance for Mr. Scrooge these past twenty years that I have forgotten about the first Mr. Scrooge. Erasing that stubborn person from my memory happened without any effort on my part. I am glad for the pleasant meeting we had several weeks ago. I didn't anticipate that my good-bye then would come to this."

Tim spoke last after pondering his most precious thoughts. "He felt so privileged to help me heal during my childhood infirmities. But, in the end, I was the one privileged to serve as his physician. In hindsight, I think he knew how our story would turn out before I did. It has left me wondering."

Tim listed natural causes on the death notice.

"Mr. Scrooge wrote his own obituary several months ago," Josiah Benham announced. "He said he wanted to have the last word in his own words, and that I should make sure it is printed without edits." Sounding professional, the erudite solicitor added, "I will deliver the copy to the newspaper tomorrow. He requested that his funeral rites be held at St. Martin-in-the-Fields three days after his death."

"Fred and Dr. Cratchit, if you come to my office tomorrow I will let you read his obituary before sending it to the Evening News for printing."

"Thank you Mr. Benham for that courtesy. I will oblige your request and stop by tomorrow after my rounds at the clinic." Tim felt honored by the solicitor's favor.

On his way home, Tim stopped by the telegraph office and sent a cable to Dover sharing details about Scrooge's funeral. The family received it after returning from the feast of St. Stephen Vespers at St. Mary of the Virgin Church. At the services, they each remembered their deceased benefactor in prayerful ways. Afterwards, Martha & Brian returned to Mercy House to visit Mr. Finley.

"Mr. Finley, we are honoring our promise for a follow-up visit. I own a security business in London," Brian began, sounding quite business-like. "Several of my clients would hire you as a maintenance employee upon my recommendation. I will contact you here at Mercy House in a week and arrange for your transportation to London for an interview." He watched tears flow down the desperate man's face. "I will take those tears as a 'Yes.'"

"I am so proud of you," Martha whispered as they made their way outdoors to the carriage. Brian turned her sentiment into a tease. "What makes you think I did that just to impress you?"

"Because," Martha pined as she slipped her arm into Brian's, "your heart is big enough for others, and not just me." To his surprise, she added, "And if you did it just for me, then I am sure it was to get a kiss which I am happy to provide."

They stood outside the carriage long enough to enjoy the delight of a strong hug and a deep kiss. Then they returned to the cottage for supper.

The next day the entire family returned on the same morning train to London, and gathered together again for the funeral of 'Uncle Ebenezer.'

After making contact with Scrooge's nephew, Fred, they each had a eulogy to prepare. The walk down memory lane would be a pleasant exercise for each Cratchit. Their stories – and their skills as storytellers would demonstrate each of their characteristic uniqueness.

Among them, the one common denominator was a desire to honor their adopted uncle as a man who radically changed his heart and values in mid-life and revealed the bountiful effects of his twenty-year transformation by leaving a trail of light for others to follow.

They each knew that the one ghost that haunted Scrooge the remaining years of his life was a ghost who enlightened his heart and guided his soul to practice charity and be kind-hearted, even to his detractors. For this reason, he was the best witness for living the spirit of Christmas all year through.

CHAPTER 26

Scrooge's Will

One week after the funeral rites, the Cratchit family gathered with Fred and his wife Catherine in the office of Josiah Benham for the reading of Scrooge's will.

Mr. Benham's opening words pleased everyone. "Mr. Scrooge asked me to announce that he left funds in escrow for the care of Mrs. Dilber." The solicitor then took each of them by surprise.

"As with his funeral, Mr. Scrooge requested that this gathering also be unconventional. According to his instructions, in place of a traditional reading of his last will and testament, he assured that you each receive a personal letter in his own handwriting. Please consider them a personal last testament for each of you. Obliging his request, I am happy to present them to you. After you read them, if you have any questions, I will be happy to answer them."

With that, the solicitor reached across his neatly-crafted paneled desk and handed the letters to those present, each sealed in a bonded envelope with the recipients' names hand-written in exquisite calligraphy.

Scrooge poured out his heart and thoughts through his pen.

From the first sentence, his nephew, Fred, became emotional by what he read.

"Before I pass on, my heart is longing to share some details about my mid-life transformation. What happened that wondrous Christmas Eve 1850 is a piece of my legacy I now trust to you, Fred, and your family. Please cherish it and pass it on to others. I am indebted to your discretion in never probing about those details. Your trust and acceptance of a new Uncle Ebenezer validated the experience as truly authentic."

"Dearest Nephew, I was visited by three spirits that Christmas Eve. The spirit of Christmas Past enabled me to visit my dearest sister, and your darling mother, Fanny. What a joy it was to see her happy face again. Her genuine concern for my sad state of a lonely life was my first awakening. The spirit of Christmas Present opened my eyes to the needs of the poor and destitute children who needed my compassion and charity to give them hope and improve their lives. This spirit did not tolerate my looking away. The more I looked, the more I was wakened to a new longing to grow a more selfless heart. The third, the Spirit-of-Christmas-yet-to-come, I feared the most. It forced me to look into an empty grave, and at a tombstone with no epitaph. It was my grave and my epitaph. Both were powerful symbols for having lived an empty and selfish life. I begged that spirit for a second chance. When I awoke that Christmas morning I made a firm promise to change."

"Dearest Fred, I am happy to leave you some tangible belongings: my house in Mayfair, my membership in the City Gentleman's Club and a 24% stake in the company. But I am more fulfilled in leaving you the intangible story of my spiritual transformation. May it find a resting place in your heart! As you and Catherine so graciously shared your love and esteem, without prejudice, I want you to know what a difference it made in nurturing my transformation the past twenty years. For all the times I failed to mention how proud I was to call you "nephew," please forgive me. For all the times you unconditionally shared your love, and gently taught me to do the same in the circle of your family life, I thank you. Your spirits of cheerfulness and contentment found a home in me and have enabled me to die a contented man. I promise to bring your needs before the throne of God and ask that abundant blessings continue to be showered upon you and yours."

Fred wiped the tears from his eyes as he shared the letter with Catherine.

Bob and Alice read his letter addressed to them quietly together.

"My esteemed friend and business partner, Robert,

"Gratitude is such an insufficient word for the patient way you nurtured my changed heart and taught me new ethical standards as a business man. My passing will be all the more peaceful because of the fond memories I have for the gentle ways you taught me to treat people with your special brand of benevolence and humility. You, Alice, and your prized children rescued me from loneliness when I most needed it, and reset my life on a path that ended with fulfillment and happiness. In the end, the Cratchits became one of my greatest treasures. I die a happier man for trusting you, and a gratified man for being so spiritually embraced every time I walked through the door of your home. Your gracious welcome opened new doors for my heart to grow in the likeness of the Christ-like Cratchit family love and kindness."

"I am happy to leave you 52% stake in the company, but, even happier sharing these heart-felt sentiments."

Alice leaned her head on her husband's shoulder. In place of tears their hearts and faces were full of smiles.

As Peter and Abigail read their letter together, Peter's emotions were touched by these words:

"The firm of Scrooge and Cratchit will continue to thrive and improve the quality of life for many thanks to your capable skills and professional direction. For the sensitive ways you added a human dimension to the business and also, to my life, I am happy to die with a heart full of pride in mentoring you and full of gratitude in honoring me with the affectionate title, Uncle Scrooge."

"Your youthful wisdom assures me that you will use a 24% stake in the company for continuing to improve the standard of living that you set as a new and noble goal for Scrooge & Cratchit."

Martha shared her letter with Brian. The manner in which Scrooge addressed her evoked a big smile.

"'Martha, my favorite adopted niece." She wiped tears from her eyes, and read on in anticipation of his parting words.

"Your confidence and assertiveness, and not my financial or moral support, are what made you a successful business women. I trust you to lean on those attributes in all your future ventures so that they result in continued good fortune for you and others."

"Never stop dreaming, my dearest Martha. Your efforts to open the business world to the women of England make you special and uphold your character to be fiercely independent. I am happy that a certain tragedy opened a door for a love story with Brain. I will pass on your personal gratitude to God for that divine intervention. Enclosed, please find the deeds to both of your stores. You justly earned them. As more of your dreams are fulfilled, I will be imploring God to help you wear your apparel designs as proudly as your trademark smile."

Tim and Julianne read his letter together. Scrooge's lines tugged at Tim's heart and stirred him to tears.

"Allowing me to care for you as Tiny Tim during your childhood disabilities was just what a grumpy man needed to mellow. My transformation was a cooperative effort between you, me and God. It was the first of many doors that opened. Whenever I walked through them with you, I discovered that being humble and childlike is the path to living a fulfilled life. Little did either of us know that Divine Providence desired then for you to become my personal physician later in life. My pride and delight in you, as your adopted 'Uncle Scrooge' has inspired me to leave an endowment of five thousand pounds for your clinic. Through this gift, I honor your legacy to me, for you have shown me how to live the spirit of Christmas all year through. Thank you for gently teaching me how kindness begets kindness; how charity begets charity. For that wisdom, my beloved Tim, I trust you to use my charitable gift to make a difference in helping to improve the lives of others. As a physician who truly cares about healing broken bodies, be assured that I will beseech the Almighty to also help you to heal their wounded souls."

As a postscript, Scrooge added,

"When I see God face-to-face, I will personally express my appreciation for inspiring you to declare, 'God bless us everyone.'

Eighteen years of vivid memories of Uncle Scrooge flashed through Tim's mind as if he were paging through a family photo album. In place of words, Julianne consoled him by kissing him on the cheek while weaving her arm tightly around his.

"Just one final item of business remains." Mr. Benham garnered everyone's attention.

"Before we depart, your Uncle Scrooge requested one final toast."

With that, the affable solicitor rang a bell. His clerk appeared with a tray of port and eleven glasses. Once they were filled, Mr. Benham raised his in tribute.

"Here's to a man we hold in high esteem. May his legacy inspire us to one day leave our own spiritual treasures for the sake of others."

They raised their glasses, and in unison, cheerfully exclaimed, "Here, here!"

CHAPTER 27

Tim & Julianne

hree weeks after the reading of the will and personal letters, Tim and Julianne returned by train to Dover. They revisited the orphanage and signed all the proper documents for the official adoption of Sophie.

During their weekend stay, the McCready's spoiled Owen and his new sister with treats and games. Tim and Julianne enjoyed brief walks along the cliffs, as the air was crisp and the winter winds were particularly strong in January 1871.

While the children slept quietly during the nights, their parents celebrated their blessings with enriching lovemaking. Their mutual respect for each other was an expectation they accomplished as a way to renew their vows to love and honor each other as husband and wife. It pushed their lovemaking beyond a functional marital activity, thereby giving God delight, the God, who, on the day of their nuptials made the two of them one.

On Sunday after lunch, Oliver took Tim Cratchit and his family to the rail station. They returned to London as a family of four.

On the train, Tim shared with Julianne his plans for the orthopedic procedures that, hopefully, would improve Owen's disability. He had scheduled them to begin in mid-week.

"In place of plaster of Paris, I plan to use splinting devices to help release pain and to realign his deformed limbs more quickly." Tim sounded clinical.

"Please go easy on him, Tim. He's still a child, and with his undeveloped immune system, anything can happen," Julianne chided her husband.

"You know I will, my dear. I will treat him not only as a patient, but also as my son," Tim countered in a way to ease her worries.

"How long do you think his recovery will last?"

"That depends much on him, my dear, his stamina and willingness to rebound," Julianne was not satisfied with Tim's reply.

"Please be more specific Tim, and give me an estimated timeline."

"My hope is that we would see some effects within three months."

Satisfied with his answer, she added, "I will do everything I can to make that happen."

The children, fascinated by the train ride, stayed wide awake. Little Owen stood by the window captivated by the fast-moving landscape outside passing before his enchanting eyes. His childish mind had no idea of what he was about to encounter in the coming week.

As Tim absorbed his son's fascination, he hoped Owen could turn the energy of this moment into the fighting spirit he would need to quickly recover from the surgery.

On Wednesday, Tim, began the first of two surgical procedures. Alice had joined Julianne in a nearby waiting room, keeping her company while stitching the hem of a new baby dress for Sophie.

Three hours later Tim emerged from the operating room, hugged his wife, and spoke the affirming words she longed to hear. "Our son is a fighter. When he awakes from the anesthesia, it will help if his mother is there." With that Tim offered his arm to Julianne. He invited his mother to follow. Within the hour Alice sent hopeful cables to everyone.

The next morning and for the rest of the week, Julianne experienced the most nauseous feelings. She shared her symptoms with Tim who whisked her into his arms and laughed:

"You're with child my dear and we must find a larger house!"

CHAPTER 28

Martha & Brian's Wedding

On a lovely spring day, one week after Easter, Brian Weller and Martha Cratchit were wedded. Keeping with tradition their nuptials were celebrated in St. Martin-in-the-Fields Church, and Martha honored her mother by wearing her wedding dress. It needed some stitching, which Alice completed in record time. Martha added the touch of "something new" with a hand-made, laced veil imported from France. Her lilies of the valley bouquet added the right color and sweet scent to her bridal looks.

Abigail consented to be her Maid of Honor. Julianne, four months pregnant, declined the invitation to be a bridesmaid. Besides, Owen, showing promising recovery from his surgeries, was still leaning on his mother for both attention and comfort.

"I don't wish to draw attention away from you on your special day Martha," her charming sister-in-law demurred. "And I'm afraid Owen might make a spectacle if I am not near."

Brian delighted his new bride on their wedding day with a grand reception at the ballroom of the Mansfield House Hotel. The one-hundred guests included Fred & Catherine, Mrs. Dilber and her niece, Colleen, the McCready's and Mr. Liam Finley who was now honorably employed at the Murdoch Manufacturing plant in East London. They dined on Bulgarian Sturgeon caviar, chicken in a white wine sauce, asparagus tips and a three-tiered wedding cake for dessert - a gift from one of Martha's customers who owned a four-star bakery.

The guests danced to the music of a string quartet and drank French champagne well into the evening. The bride and groom were the last to leave, retiring to the wedding suite, with plans to travel to Dover by train tomorrow to spend a night at the family cottage.

On Monday they would take a ferry to France and enjoy a honeymoon in Paris.

CHAPTER 29

The Newlyweds

*B*rian and Martha returned from Paris and joined the family at Bob and Alice's home for Sunday dinner. In addition to luggage they brought an assortment of gifts for every-one. Martha gave her nieces the latest porcelain dolls, and they brought Owen, the most intriguing marionette which Tim learned to operate just to enjoy the giggles from his son.

Owen had shed his leg braces and was walking with promising results. Sophie was now ten months old and showing signs of soon matching her brother by walking.

Martha brought her mother the latest sewing box invention. It had a hidden layer inside that held double the amount of her old box. She surprised her modest father with a set of velvet gloves with his initials engraved on them. Her two sister's-in-law chatted loudly about the latest silk nylon hosiery with the French designer's initials stamped on them.

Martha made Peter blush with a set of gold cufflinks with the Eiffel Tower emblazoned on them. Her brother, Tim, kissed her on the cheek for the leather business card wallet with his initials.

It was Christmas in April. The family complemented the couple on their tastes in gifts and coached out of them as many Paris stories as they could in a Sunday afternoon.

Bob and Alice couldn't have been happier hosting everyone for dinner, while sharing in the joy of Brian and Martha's safe return from their honeymoon.

"We've decided that we're going to celebrate every anniversary by visiting a different country in Europe." Martha couldn't contain her excitement as she nestled into Brian's arms with the excitement of a budding tour guide.

"My favorite memory was visiting the Louvre and seeing Paris at night from a boat on the Seine," Brian shared while planting a tender kiss on his wife's cheek.

"I'm not ready to return to work tomorrow," Martha commented, "so I may let my husband get up first, cook my breakfast and serve it to me in bed."

A noticeable wink to Brian earned a wink back from him.

The Sunday family dinner stretched out until the children showed signs of becoming grumpy. As the parents gathered them up, they were passed around for to everyone for goodnight hugs and kisses.

Brian and Martha were the last to leave. After enjoying a glass of champagne with Bob and Alice they hopped a carriage to their new home at the edge of Bayswater.

After they alighted, Brian scooped up his wife and carried her over the threshold like a stalwart husband. Their two new house maids were anticipating their arrival and had prepared their master suite. The curtains were drawn and a freshly brewed pot of hot tea was placed on a nightstand.

Martha, knowing that her menstrual clock was ticking, seduced Brian to continue the spirited lovemaking they had enjoyed in Paris. She hoped that each day following she would feel the movements of motherhood growing inside her womb.

She embraced that dream as she returned to her businesses, anxiously counting the days when she and Brian would add the blessing of another child to the Cratchit family.

Brian, in the meantime, had met another person in need, like Mr. Liam Finley, and was instrumental in helping him secure employment with another client. He felt spiritually buoyed by this new trait of charity in himself. He delighted in the new emotions it released in him and left him hungering for more. His new wife would, no doubt, help to mold him into a different and better man.

CHAPTER 30

Tim & Julianne

By the eighth month of Julianne's conceiving, Owen was bounding about like a typical two-year old son whose legs had discovered the magic of walking. His recovery was a miracle and a true testimony to Tim's surgical skills. Sophie was showing the kind of determined spirit that she needed to keep up with her highly charged older brother. The two children demanded much energy, prompting Tim to hire a governess, Christine Banks, to free Julianne from being overstressed. He wanted to make sure nothing interfered with her safe delivery.

Tim had noticed a growing passivity in his wife. She had begun to appear disengaged from him and the children. At the same time, he became concerned about an alarming jaundiced look in her features. She had not complained about the discomfort of her size during the hot summer, but Tim's medical intuition told him she was suffering in silence. He decided to break the ice with her.

"Julianne, tell me what's wrong?"

Her reply displeased him. "What makes you think something is wrong?"

"In case you've forgotten I am a doctor. I have instincts as well as training and those instincts are telling me my wife is in pain. Please talk to me."

"Well," she hesitated, "it's only a little bit of bleeding, not enough to worry about."

"Bleeding," he implored. "How long has this been happening and for how often?"

"For about a week and nearly every day," Julianne replied almost shamefully.

Standing over his wife, Tim spoke like a doctor.

"I'm calling the clinic and requesting a room. I will ask Christine, the governess, to prepare an overnight bag for you. Be ready to leave shortly."

She was not accustomed to Tim speaking to her in such a clinical tone, but as a nurse, even her own instincts, in tune with her own body, were alerting her to something serious. "Better to ere on the side of caution," she thought.

She was signed in at the clinic and resting comfortably by the time Tim returned home that evening. He checked on the children, kissed both of them on the forehead, said a quiet prayer of blessing, and slipped into bed.

It was a restless sleep missing his wife's soft breathing next to him. His mind played guessing games that swung from worry to trust. He finally dozed off, but was awakened by a knock on the bedroom door as the morning light began to pierce through the curtains. It was Christine.

"Dr. Cratchit, you have been called to the hospital."

Not knowing exactly what to expect, Tim rushed through the clinic doors and was met by Dr. Geoffrey Rhodes, a member of the surgical staff.

"Tim, can we confer in the parlor, please?" Hearing those words increased his heart rate.

Dr. Rhodes steeled himself to share some bittersweet news. "Tim I had to perform emergency surgery early this morning on your wife. You have a new born son. He is doing fine." Inhaling a deeper breath, he continued. "But I am truly sorry to tell you that Julianne did not survive. She began hemorrhaging because she had a premature separation of the placenta. We had to do an emergency C-section to save the baby. I am sorry that the bleeding was so severe, that we could not save her."

As he processed those words, Tim's face appeared paralyzed, revealing the shock of what he had just heard. He then dropped his face into both hands and wept uncontrollably. Dr. Rhodes sat beside him and embraced him, not only as a colleague, but as a dear friend whose life was now engulfed in darkness.

When his tears subsided, Tim asked his colleague to contact Dr. Manette, Julianne's father, and share the sad news. After regaining his composure, Tim asked Dr. Rhodes to see his new born son.

The five pound, six ounce baby had been cleaned and swaddled in a blue blanket. "Cratchit" had been written on a small tag and tied to his left ankle.

Tim instantly noticed that his son had his mother's dancing blue eyes and rosy cheeks. He hugged him tightly while weeping more tears. They came from a deeper, spiritual place inside where Tim felt the weight Julianne had sacrificed her life for their new son. The baby began to cry and Tim instinctively rocked him in his arms. Once he calmed down Tim caught the rhythm of the baby's calmness and began to think through all that he had to do once he left the clinic.

He stopped by his parent's house to share the news in person. Alice hugged her son as hard as her tears flowed. Bob stepped out of the parlor to weep privately. He rejoined them as mother and son discussed funeral arrangements. The usually steady Robert Cratchit needed more time to regain his composure as he sat with them in stunned silence.

"Tim, we are here for you and the children and are ready to help in any way you ask," Alice said consolingly. All Bob could do was flex his head in agreement. He eventually made a comment that Tim took to heart.

"You know, of course, the cottage is available for you and the children. It was a place of healing for Peter and Abigail and I hope it will heal you too."

"Thank you Papa," Tim said, "I will let you know when I can accept that offer."

The family rallied around Tim and his children with their special brand of Cratchit love and affection. They had been weathered by grief and loss before, and their forbearing disposition had always strengthened their bonds as a nurturing family.

Julianne's funeral was held in St. Martin-in-the-Fields. Her coffin rested in the same center aisle where she and Tim spoke their vows five years earlier.

She was buried next to Victor and within eyesight of Uncle Scrooge. The following Sunday, Tim had Julien Cratchit baptized. The son bore the name of the one person who brought fulfillment to his life as husband and father to his children.

Tim cancelled all appointments at the clinic and traveled with his children to *Clift Side Cottage*. Christine accompanied him while Oliver and Magdalena were solicitous to his every need. They cooked for him, sat with him, grieved with him and reverenced his distance when he needed time alone to walk along the cliffs. Little did the caregivers know how that solitude was the beginning of deep, inner healing for his wounded soul?

It was late September and fall was showing its colorful face. Tim felt the beginning of the autumn season's healing rays as he let a thousand memories of Julianne flash through his mind and a thousand emotions stir in his heart. Together, they evoked smiles and tears, assuring him that she was as near to him as those cherished recollections and sentiments.

By week's end, Tim had fewer tears to shed. He promised his dear wife, in a prayerful moment, to rebound from his grief and focus his energy on raising their children with all the devotion of two parents.

The following weekend, Bob and Alice traveled to Dover to strengthen Tim through the grief process and, to cheer him toward fathering their grandchildren, who will need a double portion of love from him since the death of their mother, Julianne.

CHAPTER 31

A Cratchit Family Christmas - 1871

*T*hree months after Julianne's death, the Cratchit family, including Tim and his three children, traveled to Dover for the traditional gathering at the cottage. It was the first time the family came together since the funeral. Tim's promise to his deceased wife - to father their children with singular attention and devotion - was the medicine that best worked a healing magic in him. Thanks to Christine, Tim was able to regain some balance to his dual life as a father and a physician.

With her help, his Christmas shopping list was complete and the gifts in his family stockings were neatly wrapped and tagged. In a mysterious way, Tim had become fond of Christine's company. He had dispensed with conventional etiquette and invited her to dine at the table to help feed the children. He marveled how her glowing personality added such pleasant features to the atmosphere. The more Christine and Tim talked while dining, the more he became enamored by her stark similarities to Julianne.

Christine had a disposition that was affable and pleasing. She had established a rapport with his children that was mutually affectionate. So mesmerized by Christine's skillful piano playing, Sophie was already itching to learn to play the piano-forte. She had a warm complexion and inner dispositions that made her attractive beyond her status as a governess. Tim took these attributes to heart as Christine continued to heal his loss with her company, and relieve his grief with scrupulous attention toward his children. For the sake of the children, Christine brought Tim back from the brink of solitary sorrow and awakened in him a new fondness for fatherhood.

Prior to their arrival, Martha and Brian had shared the news that she was with child and would add another grandchild to Bob and Alice's life the following summer.

Oliver and Magdalena McCready, now celebrating their tenth anniversary as caretakers of the cottage, and long considered adopted members of the Cratchit family, planned to once again enjoy a place at the table.

Peter and Abigail's life was full raising the twin girls. They silently hoped the magic of the cottage would work another miracle in the gift of a new child.

The family traditions that began on Christmas Eve day one year ago were repeated, commencing with the decorations of the house and the tree. As the wood in the fireplaces crackled with music, the family sang their traditional carols while the parents attempted to teach the words to some of the children.

Amanda and Priscilla, instead of singing, clapped loudly thinking their parents were entertaining them.

Owen attempted to mimic his father's words while Sophie chimed her own self-made tune that was off pitch. Tim and Christine howled. The children laughed. As these happy sounds bounced around the room, the energy it released was emotionally therapeutic.

Following the vigil service at St. Mary of the Virgin Church, they enjoyed a light dinner then played parlor games until everyone went to bed.

The next morning they exchanged Christmas stockings and cards while their children delighted in the return of this annual day of gift giving.

Martha surprised everyone with a comment. "This is my first Christmas as Mrs. Martha Weller. I love my new name, I love the man with whom I share it, and I love that we will soon add another child to our family. Nothing in my stocking this year could outshine these blessings, unless....." then turning to Brian she teasingly added, "I am surprised by a certain set of earrings." Everyone erupted in laughter.

Tim, inspired by Martha, followed his heart.

"I speak for everyone when I say to Martha how happy we are she and Brian found each other, and that their love story has become a happy marriage."

Everyone thought he would lose his composure by reminiscing about Julianne. Instead, his surprising words pleased them.

Gazing his eyes on Christine, Tim continued. "The loss of Juliane left me torn between coming here for Christmas or staying at home with my family. Then I realized you are my family. Over the past several months, I have also developed clarity how God and Julianne have worked hand-in-hand to heal my loss with Christine now in my life."

Everyone's eyes turned toward the governess, whose eyes were locked onto Tim. Her heart seemed to beat in rhythm with his, as Tim's fragility grew tender in the deep manner in which he shared his emotions.

"She has become more than a governess." Tim's tone had softened to a whisper. "She is a confidante, a trusted friend and, most important, a delight to my children. I am ready for a more permanent relationship, if she also desires that."

With his eyes riveted on Christine, he continued. "I have discovered that if you make me as happy as you make the children, they will grow up with a new mother knowing the special love the Cratchit's have as a family."

The silence in the parlor turned it into a hallowed room. Christine wept while smiling. She didn't wait to gain her composure.

"Tim, this is the most blessed Christmas gift I could ever receive. My heart is ready to heal yours, so yes, I accept your offer."

Tim and Christine enjoyed an abundance of warm, welcoming hugs mixed with joyful tears. The children danced around the room, not completely understanding what all the excitement was about, but nonetheless were instantly caught up in the joy of the moment.

In the dinner table blessing, Bob reverently spoke Victor, Julianne and Scrooge's names as everyone clasped hands and tightened them to strengthen their support for one another.

Martha added her own line. "As we say farewell to the deceased, thank you God for the 'hello and welcome' to Brian."

Tim followed, "And thank you God for the 'hello and welcome' to Christine."

Before dinner was served, Tim surprised the family by singing a song he had composed. He hoped it would be a new addition to the family's traditions during their annual festive gathering at the cottage.

As he chanted the words of the song in a mellow tone, the family mixed their reactions with both tears and smiles. Discouraging an applause, he ended with the words, "God bless us, everyone!"

Postscript

Tiny Tim's Christmas Song

God bless us, everyone,
The young and the old,
The timid and the bold,
God bless us everyone.

God bless us everyone,
The rich and the poor,
The ones who need less,
The ones who need more,
God bless us everyone.

God bless us everyone,
To neighbors and friends,
And strangers we send,
Greetings of cheer,
Wishes for peace,
Pass them on to join in this song,
And live it all year through,
God bless us everyone!

Acknowledgments

J am indebted to the imagination of Charles Dickens for this book. "A Christmas Carol" awakened my imagination allowing me to put to rest the central character in his popular Christmas tale and craft my own story around Bob Cratchit, his adoring family and their fortunes and tragedies after the death and funeral of Ebenezer Scrooge.

My trusted readers, Virginia Brust, and Carl Carlson offered helpful comments that embellished the story line.

My conscientious editor, Jennifer Krisp, as always, honored her two-fold role by carefully editing my grammatical mistakes, all the while making critical suggestions that polished and fine-tuned the story for the imaginations of readers.

My dependable medical consultant, Dr. Jim Clifford, helped me to express medical issues in the story in professional and simple language.

My friends, Hal and Pat Bodley, helped to quicken the completion of the manuscript by the contemplative atmosphere of their Florida home. It was just the right place for my imagination to activate and flow wildly.

I acknowledge my readers, including family and devoted friends, whose affirmation always inspires me to please your hunger for good fiction through the art of spiritually engaging storytelling. Please let me know if you think I should write a sequel to this book by bringing the Cratchits into the twentieth century.

My esteemed spiritual director, Sr. Mary Carboy, unwittingly steers my spiritual growth in ways that can be adapted to my new calling as an author. Her guidance over the past twenty years has found a resting place in my heart and my imagination.

Finally, Roy Francia and the project team at Amazon *CreateSpace* worked tirelessly to format, print and release the book in time for Christmas. They are a new gift in my life.

About the Author

Paul Mast was born in Dover (Kent County) Delaware and raised in Clayton. He attended public elementary and Catholic high school, where the seeds of a priestly vocation were nurtured. Ordained for the Diocese of Wilmington in 1972, he has post-graduate degrees from Fordham University, the Catholic University of America, and a doctorate from the University of St. Mary of the Lake in Mundelein, Illinois. In 2000, he was awarded a Certificate in Spiritual Direction from Neumann University in Aston, Pennsylvania.

Two years later, his skills were stretched to new limits as a spiritual director to survivors and parents of clergy sex abuse scandal and the ensuring scandal. It was his own version of the "Dark Night of the Soul," a spiritual metaphor of interior growth, beautifully captured as a canticle by the 16th century Spanish mystic, St. John of the Cross.

From 2008-2010, he wrote and published four articles in major Catholic periodicals regarding his experience as a spiritual director with sexual abuse survivors. These formed the backdrop for writing his first novel, *Fatal Absolution*, released in 2012 by Brighton Publishing. Following a six month sabbatical, his next book, *Street Sabbatical – Life Lessons for a Contemplative Beggar* was released in 2014. The latter is his testament to how the power of compassion toward the homeless changes hearts, helping everyone to find a home with the God of mercy.

A Cratchit Family Christmas is available in both printed and eBook editions through Amazon. If readers subscribe to the belief that the spirit of Christmas should be celebrated all year, then don't wait until the Christmas season to read it.

Currently, Paul Mast is co-authoring a murder mystery about baseball with Hal Bodley, a senior journalist for Major League Baseball and a fellow native Delawarean.

www.paulmast.com